First Love

In this tremendously moving and honest story, Judy Blume has recaptured the lustrous wonder of a first love. The physical desire at last fulfilled . . . the magic words "I love you" . . . the tender moments of sharing . . . and the certainty that these emotions will last—forever. . . .

Judy Blume knows people . . . and people in love. She portrays them with compassion and appeal, and doesn't mince words.

Forever . . . will restore to everyone the joy of falling totally in love for the first time.

"Lively, graphic . . . the story is convincing . . . explicit."—*Booklist*

Forever . . .

A NOVEL BY
Judy Blume

PUBLISHED BY POCKET BOOKS NEW YORK

POCKET BOOKS, a Simon & Schuster division of GULF & WESTERN CORPORATION
1230 Avenue of the Americas, New York, N.Y. 10020

Published by arrangement with Bradbury Press, Inc.
Library of Congress Catalog Card Number: 74-22850

ISBN: 0-671-83008-2

First Pocket Books printing August, 1976

20   19   18   17   16   15   14

Trademarks registered in the United States and other countries.

Printed in the U.S.A.

FOR RANDY
as promised . . . with love

Forever . . .

1

❦❀(1)❀❦

Sybil Davison has a genius I.Q. and has been laid by at least six different guys. She told me herself, the last time she was visiting her cousin, Erica, who is my good friend. Erica says this is because of Sybil's fat problem and her need to feel loved—the getting laid part, that is. The genius I.Q. is just luck or genes or something. I'm not sure that either explanation is 100 percent right but generally Erica is very good at analyzing people.

I don't know Sybil that well since she lives in Summit and we live in Westfield. Erica and I decided to go to her New Year's party at the last minute for two reasons—one, because that's when she invited us, and, two, we had nothing better to do.

It turned out to be a fondue party. There were maybe twenty of us sitting on the floor around a low table in Sybil's family room. On the table were a couple of big pots of steaming liquid Swiss cheese and baskets of bread chunks. Each of us had a long two-pronged fork, to spear the bread, then dip it into the cheese. It tasted pretty good. I had gotten about two bites when this guy said, "You've got some on your chin."

He was on Erica's other side, sort of leaning across her. "You want me to wipe it off?" He held out his napkin.

I couldn't tell if he was putting me on or what. So I told him, "I can wipe my own chin," and I tried to swallow the bread that was still in my mouth.

"I'm Michael Wagner," he said.

"So?" I answered, and Erica shot me a look.

She introduced herself to Michael, then tapped me on the head and said, "This idiot is my friend, Katherine. Don't mind her . . . she's a little strange."

"I noticed," Michael said. He wore glasses, had a lot of reddish-blond hair and a small mole on his left cheek. For some crazy reason I thought about touching it.

I looked away and went back to spearing chunks of bread. The guy on my other side said, "My name's Fred. I live next door to Sybil. I'm a freshman at Dartmouth." Unfortunately he was also a creep.

After a while I tuned him out but he didn't know and kept blabbing away. I was more interested in what Michael was saying to Erica. I wondered where he went to school and hoped it was some place close, like Rutgers. Erica told him that we're from Westfield, that we're seniors, and that we're spending the night at Sybil's. Then Michael introduced her to somebody named Elizabeth and I turned around in time to see him put his arm around this pale dark-haired girl sitting next to him. I pretended to be interested in Fred the Creep after all.

At midnight Sybil flashed the lights on and off and Fred wished me a Happy New Year, then tried to stuff his tongue in my mouth. I kept my lips shut tight; while he was kissing me I was watching Michael kiss Elizabeth. He was much taller than I first thought and thin, but not skinny.

After the party we helped Sybil and her parents clean up and somewhere around 3:00 a.m. we trudged upstairs to bed. Sybil conked out as soon as her head hit the pillow but Erica and I had trouble getting to sleep, maybe because we were on the floor in sleeping bags, or maybe because Sybil was snoring so loud.

Erica whispered, "Michael's a nice guy . . . don't you think so?"

"He's much too tall for you," I told her. "You'd only come up to his belly button."

"He might enjoy that."

"Oh, Erica!"

She propped herself up on an elbow and said, "You like him, don't you?"

"Don't be silly . . . we barely met." I rolled over, facing the wall.

"Yeah . . . but I can tell anyway."

"Go to sleep!"

"He asked me for your last name and your phone number."

I turned around. "He did?"

"Uh huh . . . but I guess you don't care about that." She buried herself inside her sleeping bag.

I gave her a half-hearted kick. Then we both laughed and fell asleep.

Erica and I have been friends since ninth grade. We're a good pair because she is outspoken and uninhibited and I'm not. She says she has to be that way to compensate for her size. She's just four-feet-ten—so when I said that she would come up to Michael's belly button I wasn't kidding. Everyone in her family is tiny. That's how her great-grandfather got their last name. He came to this country from Russia, not speaking a word of English. So when he stepped off the boat and the man in charge asked him his name, he didn't understand. Instead of just calling him Cohen or Goldberg, the way the immigration officers did with so many Jewish refugees, this man sized him up and wrote down *Mr. Small.* Erica swears if she ever marries she will choose someone huge so that if they decide to have children the kids will at least have a chance to grow to normal size.

Not that being little has hurt anyone in her family. Her mother is Juliette Small, the film critic. You can read her reviews in three national magazines. Because of her Erica is pos-

itive she's going to get into Radcliffe, even
though her grades aren't that hot. I have a 92
average so I almost died when I saw my college
board scores. They were below average. Erica
scored much higher than I did. She doesn't fall
apart over really important things and I'm always afraid I might. That's another difference
between us.

The phone rang at noon the next day and
woke me. Sybil jumped up and ran to answer it.
When she came back she said, "That was
Michael Wagner. He's coming over to get his
records." She yawned and flopped back on her
bed. Erica was still out cold.

I asked Sybil, "Does he go with that girl,
Elizabeth?"

"Not that I know of . . . why, are you interested?"

"No . . . just curious."

". . . because I could drop a hint if you want
me to . . ."

"No . . . don't."

"I've known him since kindergarten."

"He's in your class?"

"My homeroom."

"Oh . . . I thought he was older."

"He's a senior . . . same as us."

"Oh . . ." He seemed older. "Well . . . as long
as I'm awake I might as well get dressed," I
said, heading for the bathroom.

Sybil and I were in the kitchen when the bell

rang. I was picking raisins out of a breakfast bun, piling them in the corner of my plate. Sybil leaned against the refrigerator, spooning strawberry yoghurt out of the carton.

She answered the front door and showed Michael into the kitchen. "You remember Katherine, don't you?" she asked him.

"Sure . . . hi . . ." Michael said.

"Oh . . . hi," I said back.

"Your records are still downstairs," Sybil told him. "I'll get them for you."

"That's okay," Michael said. "I'll get them myself."

A few seconds later he called, "Who's K.D.?"

"Me," I answered. "Some of those albums are mine." I went downstairs and started going through the pile. "Are yours marked?"

"No."

I was making a stack of K.D.s when he said, "Look . . ." and grabbed my wrist. "I came over here because I wanted to see you again."

"Oh, well . . ." I saw my reflection in his glasses.

"Is that all you can say?"

"What am I supposed to say?"

"Do I have to write the script?"

"Okay . . . I'm glad you came over."

He smiled. "That's better. How about a ride? My car's out front."

"My father's coming to pick me up at 3:00. I have to be back by then."

"That's okay." He was still holding my wrist.

2

Everyone says that Erica has insight. I suppose that's how she knew I was interested in Michael before I admitted it to anyone, including myself. It's true that I come on strong with my sarcastic act sometimes, but only when I'm interested in a guy. Otherwise I can be as nice and friendly as they come. Erica says that means I'm insecure. Maybe she's right—I just don't know.

A few minutes after we pulled out of Sybil's driveway we drove past Overlook Hospital. I told Michael I work there every Thursday after school. "I'm a Candy Striper," I said, "and I was born there too."

"Hey . . . so was I," he said.

"What month? Maybe we slept next to each other in the nursery."

"May," he said.

"Oh . . . I'm April." I sneaked a look at him. His profile was nice but I could see he'd broken his nose more than once. His hair reminded me of Erica's golden retriever, Rex. It was exactly the same color.

Michael drove down the hill into the Watchung Reservation. "I used to ride here," he said.

I pictured him on a Honda XL 70.

"I had this one favorite . . . Crab Apple . . . until the time she threw me and I fractured my arm."

"Oh . . . a horse!" I laughed.

He glanced over at me.

"I thought you meant a motorcycle," I said. "I've never ridden a horse."

"I figured that . . . you're not the horsey type."

Was that good or bad? "How can you tell?" I asked.

"I just can."

"What else can you tell?"

"I'll let you know later." He smiled at me and I smiled back. "You have nice dimples," he said.

"Thanks . . . everyone in my family has them."

He parked the car and we got out. It was cold and windy but the sun was shining. We walked down to the lake. It was partly frozen. Michael picked up a handful of stones and tossed them across the water. "What are you doing next year?"

"Going to college."

"Where?"

"I don't know yet," I said. "I applied to Penn

State, Michigan and Denver. I have to see where I'm accepted. What about you?"

"University of Vermont, I hope. Either there or Middlebury." Michael took my hand and pulled off my mitten, which he shoved into his pocket. Holding hands, we started walking around the lake.

"I wish it would snow," he said, squeezing my fingers.

"Me too."

"You ski?"

"No . . . I just like snow."

"I love to ski."

"I know how to water ski," I told him.

"That's different."

"Are you good . . . at skiing, I mean?"

"You might say that. I could probably teach you."

"To ski?"

"Yeah."

"That'd be nice."

We walked all the way to the Trailside Museum and had a look inside, before Michael checked his watch and said, "We better head back."

"Already?"

"It's after 2:00."

My teeth were chattering and I knew that my cheeks would be bright red from the wind. I didn't mind though. My father says I look good that way—very healthy.

When we were back in the car I rubbed my

hands together, trying to get warm, while Michael started up the engine. It stalled a few times. When it finally caught he pumped the gas. "I better give it a minute to make sure," he said.

"Okay."

He turned to face me. "Can I kiss you, Katherine?"

"Do you always ask first?"

"No . . . but with you I don't know what to expect."

"Try me . . ." I said.

He took off his glasses and put them on the dashboard.

I wet my lips. Michael kept looking at me. "You're making me nervous," I told him. "Stop staring."

"I just want to see what you look like without my glasses."

"Well?"

"You're all blurred."

We both laughed.

Finally he kissed me. It was a nice kiss, warm but not sloppy.

Before he let me out at Sybil's house, Michael stopped the car and kissed me again. "You're delicious," he said.

No boy had ever told me that. As I opened the car door all I could think of to say was, "See you . . ." but that wasn't at all what I meant.

3

"I met a very nice boy," I told my mother that night, "even though he's still in high school." Mom was in her bathroom, trimming her toenails. "He has this reddish-blond hair and wears glasses. He likes to ski."

"What's his name?" Mom asked.

"Michael Wagner . . . isn't that a nice name?"

She looked up and smiled at me. "It must have been a good party."

"It was okay . . . I'm seeing him Friday night . . . and Saturday too."

"Where's he from?"

"Summit . . . he goes to school with Sybil. Can I borrow your nail scissors when you're done? I can't find mine."

"Here . . ." Mom handed them to me. "But don't forget to return them this time."

"I won't."

My mother's name is Diana—Diana Danziger. It sounds like she should be a movie star or something. Actually, she's a librarian, in charge of the children's room at the public library. Mom is naturally thin, so she can eat four cupcakes at one sitting or polish off as much beer as she wants. We are exactly the same size—five-feet-six and 109 pounds—but she is sort of flat chested and never wears a bra.

While I was cutting my toenails my sister, Jamie, came into my room, holding up a pair of jeans. "I embroidered them while you were at Sybil's. What do you think?"

"They're just great," I told her. "They're fantastic!"

"Want me to do a pair of yours?"

"Would you?"

"Sure."

"By next weekend?"

"Yeah . . . I guess I could."

"Jamie . . ." I said, hugging her, "you are an absolute angel!"

Jamie is in seventh grade and looks a lot like me but her eyes are fabulous—big and round—and if you look into them you get the feeling you can see deep inside her. Sometimes they seem very dark, with just a rim of green and other times they sparkle and are greenish-gray all over, like my grandfather's. The rest of us have ordinary brown eyes but my father's brows grow straight across the bridge of his nose. He told me that when he was in college he used to shave them up the center.

Jamie untangled herself from me. "What's next weekend?" she asked.

"I'm seeing someone I met last night," I told her, "and the truth is, I don't know how I'm going to live through this week."

"You mean you're in love again?"

"I have never been in love."

"What about Tommy Aronson?"

"That wasn't love . . . that was childish infatuation."

"You said it was love . . . I remember."

"Well, I didn't know anything then."

"Oh."

"Some day you'll understand."

"I doubt it," Jamie said.

I wish she hadn't brought up the subject of Tommy Aronson, because I did like him a lot last year, but only for a few months. Now he's at Ohio State and the news I get is he's so busy making it with every female on campus he may flunk out. I hope he does. Sex was all he was ever interested in, which is why we broke up— because he threatened that if I wouldn't sleep with him he'd find somebody who would. I told him if that was all he cared about he should go right ahead. So he did. Her name was Dorothy and she turned up in my English class this year.

Michael was different from Tommy Aronson right away. He called me every night.

"Hi . . . it's me, Michael," he said on Tuesday.

"Hi . . ."

"I'm sitting on the bed with this beautiful fifteen-year-old . . ."

"Oh?"

"Yeah . . . her name's Tasha . . . she's gray and furry and she's got a beard but I love her anyway."

I laughed. "A schnauzer?"

"How'd you guess?"

"The beard. Isn't fifteen kind of old for a dog?"

"In people years she'd be 105."

"Can she still get around?"

"Sure . . . she just doesn't bark much anymore. Wait a second and I'll put her on . . . say hello to Katherine, Tasha . . . don't be shy . . ."

"Hello, Tasha . . ." I said. "Arf . . . arf . . ."

The next night I asked Michael if he plays tennis.

"Not really . . . why, do you?"

"Uh huh . . . I'm on the school team," I said.

"Oh, a jock, huh?"

"Hardly . . . just that and modern dance . . ."

"A dancer too?"

"Um . . . sort of . . ."

"You jump around wearing one of those things?"

"What things?"

"You know . . ."

"A leotard, you mean?"

"That's it."

"I wear one."

"I'd like to see that."

"Some day, maybe . . . if you're lucky."

On Thursday night he said, "Did I tell you I'm trying to get my ski instructor's pin by next year?"

"No . . ."

"Yeah, I am. Do you by any chance like spinach?"

"Ugh, no . . . why, do you?"

"It's only my favorite food."

"Like Popeye?"

"Like Popeye."

"In that case, maybe I'll try to develop a taste for it . . . but I can't promise . . ."

"Hey . . . you know tomorrow's Friday?"

"I know."

"How's 7:30?"

"Fine."

"Well . . . see you then . . ."

"See you then. Oh, Michael . . ."

"Yeah?"

"I'll be ready."

I was nervous about seeing him again. On Friday, right after school, I washed my hair. I couldn't eat any dinner. My parents gave me a couple of funny looks but neither one said anything. Jamie had embroidered my jeans with tiny mushrooms and I'd bought a light blue sweater to go with them. I once read that boys like light blue on a girl better than any other color. I was ready half an hour early.

As soon as I opened the door we both started

talking at the same time. Then we looked at each other, laughed, and I knew it was going to be all right between us.

Michael followed me into the living room.

My mother and father were stretched out on the floor, hooking a rug—Jamie's latest design. She paints the canvas and the three of us put in the colors. Hooking rugs is very easy and lots of fun but I wasn't sure what Michael would think and for a minute I was sorry I hadn't asked them to turn on the TV and just sit there.

"Michael," I said, "I'd like you to meet my parents." Then, "Mom . . . Dad . . . this is Michael Wagner."

My father stood up and he and Michael shook hands. Mom pushed her glasses up on her head so she could get a good look at him. She can see only close up when she's wearing them.

Michael cleared his throat and looked around. "This is really something," he said.

My mother was pleased. She said, "Thanks . . . we like it too."

I have to explain about our house. It's very ordinary on the outside but on the inside it's really something, like Michael said. All the walls are painted white and are hung with a million of Jamie's paintings and tapestries which are all done in bright, beautiful colors. Her artwork is not your everyday twelve-year-old's. She is what is called a gifted child. When you combine my mother's plants with Jamie's artwork you don't need anything else—our furniture is very plain and it's all kind of beige so that you don't notice it, which is the whole idea.

Jamie came tearing down the stairs then, yelling, "Is he here yet? Did I miss him?" When she saw Michael she blushed. "Oh . . . he's here."

Michael laughed.

"This is my sister, Jamie," I told him, ". . . in case you hadn't already guessed."

"Hi, Jamie," Michael said.

"Hi," she answered.

In many ways Jamie is still a little girl. She looks up to me—at least that's what my parents say. And I think they might be right. It took a long time for me to realize that, but when I did it helped me get over being jealous of all her talents. Not that I don't get a pang now and then, like when Michael admired everything she's made and I knew he wasn't just saying it to make her feel good but that he was really impressed.

As soon as I got into my jacket Michael and I left. We went to the Blue Star Cinema and held hands. All I could think about was later and being alone with him.

After the movie we stopped off at a diner on Route 22. When we'd finished eating Michael said, "Do you know any place to park around here?"

"No," I told him. "But we could go back to my house."

"Your parents won't mind?"

"They'd rather have me bring my friends home than sit in a car somewhere."

"Okay . . . it's back to your house, Katherine."

I really do know where people go to park. There's a dark, dead-end street not far from where I live and there is also the golf course and the hill. Erica lives on the hill. She's always finding used rubbers in the street. I can't understand how someone could just throw a thing like that out a car window and forget about it.

My mother and father talked to me about parking when I first started going with guys who drove. They explained how it isn't safe, not because of anything we might do, but because there are a lot of crazies in this world and they have been known to prey on couples who are out parking. So I've always invited my boyfriends home.

We have a den on one side of the living room that's very private. It's got a door and everything. It's small but there's a fireplace with two tilt-back chairs in front of it, a stereo built into the wall unit and a comfortable sofa under the windows, with the kind of cushions you sink into. There's a big, beautiful hooked rug on the floor with a lion's face in the middle.

My mother and father go to bed early—between 10:00 and 11:00, unless they go out or have company. They were already asleep when I got home with Michael. I have no curfew but I am supposed to let them know when I get in, and that I'm okay. I tiptoe upstairs and whisper, "Psst . . . I'm home." Usually my father hears me and mumbles something. Then he rolls over and goes back to sleep.

Michael had turned on the stereo and was poking the fire when I came back downstairs. I closed the den door and sat down on the sofa. He took off his glasses, put them on the side table, and joined me. We put our arms around each other and I lifted my face. But after a short kiss he said, "You brushed your teeth?"

"Yes."

"You taste like toothpaste."

"Is that bad?" I asked.

"I don't mind . . . but it makes your mouth cold."

"It does?"

"Yeah."

"I didn't know that."

"It's okay . . . it'll warm up in a minute."

"I hope so."

When we kissed again Michael used his tongue. I wanted him to.

We sat together on the sofa for an hour. Michael moved his hands around on the outside of my sweater but when he tried to get under it I said, "No . . . let's save something for tomorrow."

He didn't pressure me. He kissed my cheek, then my ear, and whispered, "Are you a virgin?"

No boy had ever come right out and asked me

that—not even Tommy Aronson. I told Michael, "Yes, I am . . . does it matter?"

"No . . . but it's better if I know."

"Well, now you know."

"Don't get defensive, Katherine. It's nothing to be ashamed of."

"I'm not ashamed."

"Okay then . . . let's just forget it. I like you just the same. I like being with you."

"I like being with you too."

It occurred to me in the middle of the night that Michael asked if I was a virgin to find out what I expected of him. If I hadn't been one then he probably would have made love to me. What scares me is I'm not sure how I feel about that.

4

ᴄᴏ()ᴏᴗ

My father is a pharmacist. He owns Danziger's Drugs in town and Danziger's Two in Cranford. He is also very big on physical activity. He works out at a gym four times a week and plays tennis every morning from 7:30 to 8:30.

I suppose I get my physical coordination from him. I've been playing tennis since I was eight. I play a good game. One of Jamie's goals is to play tennis like me, even though when it comes to sports she is hopeless. I think she should stick to the things she does well. I mean, you can't excel at everything. I know better than to want to be great at music and art, like Jamie. I'm realistic about myself. I think a person has to be.

My father keeps warning my mother that if she doesn't start to work out at the gym soon, she'll wind up with flabby thighs. I can't imagine my mother with flab anywhere but just a few months ago I overheard her divorced friend tell her, "You really should take better

29

care of yourself, Diana. Roger is so attractive and he's at that dangerous age."

"Bullshit," my mother answered. But when I was nine and Jamie was four we had this baby-sitter who had a *thing* for Dad. As soon as my parents left the house she would run up to his closet and touch all his things. She even smelled some of them. Finally, I told Mom and we never had that sitter again.

During Christmas vacation when both of our stores are fantastically busy I help out selling cosmetics and Jamie sometimes gift wraps. You wouldn't believe how many people buy last minute Christmas presents. They'll take absolutely anything they can get their hands on.

In January business slows down and toward the end of the month my parents go away for a week, usually to Mexico. Then my grandparents come to stay with us. They are my mother's parents. My father's are both dead. My grandmother, Hallie Gross, once ran for Congress, but she lost. She and my grandfather practice law together in New York. Since Grandpa had his stroke he hasn't handled any cases but he still goes to the office every day. My Uncle Howard, who is my mother's brother, really runs the show. Grandma is too busy with politics and Planned Parenthood and NOW to see many clients. I can't believe that she is almost seventy years old.

The night before my parents left for their vacation they said it would be all right for me to have some friends over. Michael brought Artie Lewin and I asked Erica. One thing about Erica—you never have to worry about her getting along with anyone. You can fix her up with the worst guy in the world and she'll act like he's someone special. That doesn't mean she'll make out with him but she will find something to talk about and he'll always call and ask to see her again. Grandma says Erica would make a great politician.

Artie turned out to be my height, with a good build, nice speckled eyes and terrific teeth. He was perfect for Erica. She goes for guys with good teeth.

For a while we all sat around and talked, then Artie said, "How about a game of backgammon?"

"We don't have it," I told him.

"Never mind that," Artie said, "I have mine in the car."

"You brought it with you?" Erica asked.

"I always bring it along . . . just in case."

"In case . . . what?" Erica said.

"In case we run out of things to do. But if you don't play backgammon I have Monopoly, Clue, Yahtzee, chess . . ."

"Scrabble," Michael added.

"Oh yeah . . . Scrabble . . ."

"A regular traveling game show," Erica said.

"So what do you say?" Artie asked.

"Backgammon," Erica told him.

"Great . . . don't go away . . . I'll be right back."

We laughed as Artie ran out to the car to get his set.

Erica's a whiz at backgammon. She plays a very offensive game. But by 10:00 she was down two games to Artie and the challenge was on.

Michael and I sat on the sofa. I reached for his hand and traced the lines of his palm with my finger. "Very interesting," I said.

"You read palms?" he asked.

"Sometimes."

"What do you see?"

"Oh . . . a long life line . . . that's good. And over here I see a girl with brown hair . . ."

"I see one too," he said, looking into my eyes.

My insides turned over. I moved as close to him as I could. I rested my head on his shoulder and held onto his hand. He put his arm around me.

At 10:30 we convinced Artie and Erica to take a break and go out for pizza and when we got back Mom and Dad had gone to sleep. Michael built us a fire in the den and we turned out all the lights. Erica and Artie sat together in a tilt-back chair but after a few minutes they got up and went into the other room, closing the door behind them.

"I love your hair," Michael whispered, burying his face in it. "It always smells so good." He kissed my ears, my neck and my lips. Then he got up and walked across the room. "Lie down next to me, Kath . . . here, in front of the fire."

This was the fifth week in a row we'd seen each other. I'd asked him to go slow with me and he promised he would. I stretched out beside him. I felt his body against mine. He reached under my sweater and tried to unhook my bra but he had a lot of trouble and I wondered if I should help him out or just lie still and wait. He got it undone. His hands were cold at first but I didn't flinch. I pressed myself as tight against him as I could.

"I'm crazy about you." He touched me and we kissed until the same record had played three times. But when he fumbled with the snap on my jeans I sat up and said, "No . . . not now . . . not with them in the other room."

Michael rolled over onto his stomach and kind of groaned. I bent down and stroked his hair. "You're not mad, are you?"

"No."

"You're sure?"

"Yeah . . . but this is really rough . . ."

"I know it . . ."

"Give me a minute by myself, okay?" he asked.

"Sure." I needed a minute alone too. It wasn't easy to stop.

I opened the den door slowly, not sure what I would find on the other side, but Erica and Artie were sitting at the kitchen table, playing Monopoly. Erica never loses at that game. She steals from the bank.

"Well . . ." Erica said, looking me over, "we were beginning to give up on you two."

"We . . . uh . . ."

Erica held up her hand. "Please . . . spare us the gory details."

"Where's my buddy?" Artie asked.

"Oh . . . he'll be right out."

I went upstairs to the bathroom and splashed cold water on my face. If Artie and Erica hadn't been there I doubt that I'd have stopped Michael from unbuttoning my jeans. But I'm not sure. Now I wanted the boys to go home.

Michael had his jacket on when I came downstairs. "We have to take off now," he said. "It's late . . . see you next week." He gave me a quick kiss.

I was sorry I'd invited Erica to spend the night. While she was getting ready for bed I said, "I think I forgot to turn out the light in the den . . . I'll be right back . . ." I ran downstairs. I'd already put out all the lights but Erica didn't know. I sat down on the rug where Michael and I had been together. Our rug, I thought. I ran my hands over it. It was still warm.

When I got back to my room Erica was in bed. "Must have been a lot of lights on," she said.

"Yeah." I looked at her. "Did you like Artie?"

"He's nice," she said, "but I think he's shy or something. He didn't try to kiss me."

"He didn't seem shy."

"I know . . . that's what's funny . . . I don't have bad breath or anything, do I?" She sat up, leaned over and breathed hard in my face.

"You smell fine."

"Maybe he wasn't attracted to me. Maybe he thinks I'm too little."

"It probably wasn't anything like that."

"He could be inexperienced, I suppose," Erica said. "If that's the case I could teach him. I really wouldn't mind . . . I love his teeth."

I pulled on my nightshirt. "I knew you would."

"Tell me about Michael, Kath."

"What about him?"

"Is he any good?"

"Uh huh . . . he knows what he's doing."

"Do you love him?"

"I like him a lot . . . that's all I know right now." I turned out the bedroom light. I wasn't going to say I loved Michael yet. I was too quick to think I'd loved Tommy Aronson and he and I never even got to be friends. I already knew Michael better than I'd ever known Tommy. And the way I'd felt about Tommy last year was nothing compared to what I felt for Michael.

"Are you still a virgin?" Erica asked.

"Yes."

"Is he?"

"I don't know . . . I haven't asked."

"I've been thinking," Erica said, "that it might not be a bad idea to get laid before college."

"Just like that?"

"Well . . . I'd have to be attracted to him, naturally."

"What about love?"

"You don't need love to have sex."

"But it means more that way."

"Oh, I don't know. They say the first time's never any good anyway."

"Which is why you should at least love him," I said.

"Maybe . . . but I'd really like to get it over with."

"What's the point?"

"I'm always thinking about it . . . wondering who's going to be the one . . . like tonight, I kept picturing myself with Artie . . . and in school I sit in class thinking how it would be with every guy . . ."

"Really?"

"Yes . . . even the teachers . . . I wonder about them too . . . especially Mr. Frazier, since he never zips his fly all the way. Tell the truth, Kath . . . don't you think about it?"

"Well, sure . . . but I want it to be special."

"You're a romantic," Erica said. "You always have been. I'm a realist."

"You're starting to sound like some kind of professor . . ."

"I mean it," Erica said, "we look at sex differently . . . I see it as a physical thing and you see it as a way of expressing love."

"That's not completely true . . ."

"Maybe not . . . but that's the picture I get."

"Well, you don't know Michael . . . that's all I can say."

5

Another thing about Jamie is, she can cook. Not hotdogs and hamburgers like me, but real, honest-to-god gourmet stuff. When my grandparents came to stay with us the first week in February, Jamie did all the cooking. Every night, before they went to sleep, Grandma and Jamie pored over cookbooks deciding on the menu for the following day. While Jamie was at school Grandma did the grocery shopping. Once she drove all the way back to New York to get special spices for a recipe. After school they both went to work in the kitchen, preparing the feast. Jamie gave Grandma small jobs, like chopping shallots, but did all the important things herself. Since they went to so much trouble they usually invited guests for dinner. My grandmother knows everybody, from the mayor to the man behind the counter at the fish market, so you never could tell who might turn up.

While they cooked, Grandpa would wander into the kitchen, lifting lids off pots and sniffing inside. Since his stroke he walks with a cane and has trouble talking. He can't always get the right words out. It's sad to see him struggle over a simple sentence and hard to keep from trying to finish it for him. My mother was very close to Grandpa while she was growing up and now when they're together I can see how painful it is for her to watch him. But my grandmother treats him the same as always, like there's nothing wrong at all.

I've heard that people who come from happy homes, with parents who really care about each other, like my grandparents, tend to have good marriages themselves. And I believe it. My mother and father are certainly the happiest married couple I know. They really enjoy being together, which doesn't mean they agree on everything, because they definitely don't. But after an argument they laugh about it and I like that.

On Thursday night of the week my parents were away Michael picked me up at the hospital and drove me home. "What floor do you work on?" he asked.

"Third," I told him, "in geriatrics."

"Geriatrics . . . that's old people, isn't it?"

"Yes."

"Why'd they put you in there?"

"I requested it."

"How come?"

"Oh . . . it's a long story . . ."

"I'm listening"

"It's hard to explain . . ."

"Come on . . . I'm interested . . . really . . ."

"Well . . . when I was a little kid my father's mother lived in an old age home in Trenton and every Sunday we had to drive down to see her and I always wound up crying . . . you sure you want to hear this?"

"Uh huh . . ."

"Okay . . . so my parents would explain it by saying I was just overtired from the long ride . . . but the truth was, I hated the place. Just the smell of it made me feel sick . . . you know?"

"Go on . . ."

"Well . . . I never really knew my grandmother . . . as a person, that is . . . she was just some old lady with crooked fingers and wrinkled skin and I was kind of afraid of her . . . and of the other old people too . . . I was scared that one of them might grab me and hide me in a closet and my parents wouldn't be able to find me . . . ." I looked over at Michael before I went on. "Then, when I was about seven, my grandmother died, and I was glad . . . because we didn't have to go to Trenton anymore . . . God, I've never told anybody this story . . ." I took a deep breath. ". . . so anyway, when my grandfather—that's my mother's father . . . you'll meet him tonight—when he got sick last year and I went to the hospital to visit him I realized that he was old too . . . but I wasn't afraid of him . . . because I loved him. I guess this doesn't

make much sense to you . . . but that's why I
asked to work in geriatrics . . ."

"It makes a lot of sense," Michael said.

"Look . . . don't get the wrong idea . . . I'm no
Florence Nightingale . . . and I'm not big on
blood and guts . . . I don't do much for the pa-
tients . . . just deliver the mail and flowers . . .
and bring water and adjust beds . . . nothing
special . . . but it makes me feel good . . ."

"It makes you look good too."

I pulled my coat around me and laughed. "I
always feel funny in my uniform . . . like I'm
dressed for a part in a play or something . . ."

"Say . . . that reminds me . . . our school play's
in two weeks. Artie's got the lead."

"Artie . . . I can't picture him on stage."

"Why not?"

"I don't know . . . he doesn't seem like the
type . . ."

"You'd be surprised."

"He's so self-conscious."

"Artie . . . self-conscious . . . never."

"Not with you . . ." I said.

"You mean with Erica!"

"Uh huh."

"I don't know about that . . ."

"Well, anyway, I'd like to see him in the
play."

"Good . . . and there's a party after it . . . at
Elizabeth Hailey's house."

"Didn't you used to go with her?"

"Not exactly."

"But New Year's Eve . . ."

"We were together but it wasn't anything special."

"Still . . . won't you feel funny bringing me to her house?"

"Why should I?" Michael took one hand off the wheel and reached for mine. "We go together, don't we? It's no big secret or anything." I tightened my fingers around his.

When we got to my house Grandma, Grandpa and Jamie were entertaining the DiNizios, from next door—I used to babysit for their kids—and Mr. and Mrs. Salamandre, our butcher and his wife. I introduced Michael to everyone, then Grandma insisted we join them for dessert, which was a chocolate mousse with almondine sauce. Michael said it was the greatest thing he'd ever tasted and Jamie positively beamed.

After that Michael had to leave and I had to study for a Spanish test. I walked him to his car and got in for a minute. We kissed goodbye.

Later, Grandma said, "He's a nice boy, Kath."

"I know."

"Intelligent."

"Uh huh."

"Attractive, too."

"I agree."

"Just be careful . . . that's my only advice."

"Of what?"

"Pregnancy."

"Grandma!"

"And venereal disease."

"Really . . ."

"Does it embarrass you to talk about it?"

"No, but . . ."

"It shouldn't."

"But listen, Grandma . . . we aren't sleeping together."

"Yet," Grandma said.

In the old days girls were divided into two groups—those who did and those who didn't. My mother told me that. Nice girls didn't, naturally. They were the ones boys wanted to marry. I'm glad those days are over but I still get angry when older people assume that everyone in my generation screws around. They're probably the same ones who think all kids use dope. It's true that we are more open than our parents but that just means we accept sex and talk about it. It doesn't mean we are all jumping into bed together. I was really surprised that Grandma thought Michael and I are lovers, in the true sense.

On the final night my grandparents stayed with us they had tickets to a concert at Lincoln Center. I said they should go and that I would stay home with Jamie and ask Michael over to keep us company. Jamie liked the idea of cooking something special for him. Finally, Grandma said, "I've checked with the DiNizios and they'll be home and you know the number in case of fire, don't you . . ."

"Yes," I said.

"Then I guess it's all right for us to go."

"I've been babysitting since ninth grade," I said.

"I know . . . I know . . . but with your mother and father away I feel responsible."

"Everything will be fine. You and Grandpa don't have to worry . . . just enjoy yourselves."

Jamie cooked all day. She made veal marsala, spinach salad and lemon chiffon pie. Michael devoured everything. When we were done I told her we'd do the dishes and she went downstairs to practice the piano. She has a kind of studio down there, where she can work on her music and her artwork undisturbed.

Michael and I loaded the dishwasher but there wasn't any room left for the pots and pans so I filled the sink with hot sudsy water and said, "I'll wash and you dry." I handed him a dish towel.

"Aren't you afraid of dishpan hands?" he asked.

"Nope . . . are you?"

"Oh, sure . . ." He held out his hands, pretending to admire them. "I only use Ivory . . . that's why everyone thinks I'm eighteen instead of thirty-eight. My hands don't give me away."

"You idiot!" I flicked some soap bubbles at him.

"Hey . . ." He reached into the sink, picked up a handful of suds and threw them at me.

So I tossed some more at him and he tossed

them back and we had a terrific water fight until both of us were dripping and laughing hysterically. I cried, "No more, Michael . . . please . . ."

He wiped off his face with the dish towel, then started snapping it at me. "Work, slave, work . . . clean up this mess."

"Stop it . . ." I told him, jumping away, but he kept snapping the towel at my legs. I ran around the kitchen, shrieking, with Michael chasing me, only now he was aiming the towel at my behind.

"I'm going to get you," I said, reaching into the broom closet. I came out with the feather duster and tickled his face.

"You'll have to pay for that," Michael said, grabbing my wrists. I dropped the feather duster as he pushed me against the counter. He took off his glasses before he kissed me.

"Why do you always do that?" I asked him after.

"Did you every try to kiss with glasses on?"

"No."

"Well . . . they get in your way," he said. "Your hair's all wet."

"So's yours." I reached up and rumpled it. "We better dry off."

We went upstairs to the bathroom. When I looked in the mirror I was surprised. "Hey . . . I really do have soapy hair."

"Just remember who started it," Michael said.

"Hmph!"

"I'll shampoo it for you, if you want."

"You will?"

"Yeah."

"In the sink?"

"Unless you prefer the shower."

"Very funny."

"Well?"

"Okay." I handed him the shampoo and bent over the sink.

He did a good job on my hair and when he was done I wrapped a towel around my head, then shampooed him. We rubbed each other's heads until they were barely damp.

"I have to change my shirt," I said. "It's drenched."

"Go ahead."

I walked down the hall to my bedroom. Michael was right behind me. "I'll just be a minute," I told him as I started to close my door.

But he pushed it back open. "I'll stay."

"Oh, Michael . . . come on."

"I promise, I won't touch." He closed the door behind him.

I took a sweater and bra out of my dresser drawer while Michael bounced up and down on my bed. "Very nice," he said, "firm but not too hard."

"I'm glad you approve."

"Did you know that soft mattresses are no good for making love?"

"Michael . . ."

"Really . . . I mean it."

"That's very interesting . . . now would you please leave so I can change."

"Are you ashamed of your body, Katherine?"

"No . . . of course not."

"Then what's the difference if I stay?"

"Oh . . ." I shook my head at him, turned away and unbuttoned my shirt. I pulled it off and unhooked my bra, which was also wet. Then I hesitated for a minute and slipped that off too. I reached for my dry bra and put it on. All that time neither of us said anything.

Then Michael was behind me.

"You promised . . ." I reminded him.

"I'll hook it for you . . . that's all."

"Don't bother."

"It's no trouble." But instead of hooking it he slid his hands around to my breasts and kissed the back of my neck.

"Please, Michael . . . don't."

"Why not, Kath?"

"Because . . ."

There was a knock at my door then and Jamie called, "What are you two doing in there? The kitchen's a mess and it's almost time for the 9:00 movie."

"Coming . . ." I answered, hooking my bra and pulling on my sweater. Then I turned to Michael and whispered, "That's why . . ."

"Excuses, excuses," he said.

"Ha ha."

We finished up in the kitchen and sat in the

den with Jamie, watching the Saturday night movie on TV. When it was over Michael kissed us both goodnight, me on the lips and Jamie on the cheek. She was still touching her face when I went in to tell her goodnight.

"I think Michael is the nicest boy in the whole world," she said.

"That makes two of us."

"I wish he had a younger brother."

"That would be fun . . . but he doesn't."

"Kath . . ."

"Hmmm?"

"What were you two doing in your bedroom?"

"Nothing . . . Michael just wanted to see it."

"Come on, Kath . . . I won't tell anybody."

"There's nothing to tell."

"I know all about sex."

"Congratulations!"

"Were you fucking?"

"Jamie!"

"That's not a bad word . . . hate and war are bad words but fuck isn't."

"I never said it was."

"So were you?"

"No . . . I wasn't . . . but even if I was I wouldn't tell you."

"Why not?"

"Because it's none of your damn business . . . that's why."

"Oh wow . . ." she said, clucking her tongue, "your generation is so hung up about sex."

6

"How'd it go with Artie?" I asked Erica on Monday. We were in zoology, classifying mollusks.

"I'll tell you how it went," Erica said, ". . . it didn't!"

"He never showed up?"

"Oh, he showed up all right."

"So?"

"Still nothing . . . not even a kiss."

"Weird."

"And I'm sure he likes me. He asked me to his school play . . . he's got the lead."

"I heard. I'm going with Michael."

"I know . . . Artie said he'll arrange for you two to bring me."

"Fine."

"If he doesn't try anything after the play I'm going to do something about it. I can't sit around waiting forever."

Mr. Kolodny looked up from his desk. "Will

you girls in the back please stop talking and get
to work."

I pulled out a sheet of notebook paper, wrote
Like what? and shoved it at Erica.

She wrote back, *Something drastic!*

On the night of the play Michael, Erica and
I sat together in the fourth row of the auditor-
ium at Summit High. The play was *Butterflies
Are Free* and Artie played the blind boy trying
to make it on his own. Michael was right—
Artie really surprised me. He was as good as a
professional. Somehow, he seemed different on
stage—more sure of himself. He made me forget he was Artie Lewin, game freak.

Sybil played his mother and Elizabeth played
his girlfriend but they couldn't compare to Artie.
It didn't help that Sybil looked fatter than ever
and kept fidgeting with her gray wig. Elizabeth's costume consisted of the world's skimpi-
est bikini and when she first came on stage
Erica nudged me with an elbow. For some stupid reason I felt I had to say something to Michael—something to show I'm not the jealous
type. So I leaned over and whispered, "She's
very pretty." How did I ever think up such a
clever remark?

"Uh huh," Michael said.

When the play ended Artie got a standing
ovation.

"I had no idea . . ." Erica said over and over.
"I just can't believe it."

"Me neither."

"I told you," Michael said. "It's the most important thing in his life."

As I watched Artie take another bow I could see that Michael was right again.

We tried to go backstage but there were two teachers in charge of keeping everyone out since the custodians were anxious to lock up the school for the night. Erica said she'd wait for Artie and that we should go on to the party.

I wasn't looking forward to going to Elizabeth's house and facing her close up. But there was nothing I could do about it without being obvious. Besides, how would Artie feel if his best friend didn't show?

Elizabeth's house was on a street a lot like mine. Her mother answered the door.

"Michael . . ." Mrs. Hailey said, "it's so nice to see you again."

"Mrs. Hailey . . . this is Katherine Danziger," Michael told her.

"Hello," I said.

"Come in . . . come in . . ." Mrs. Hailey said, looking me over. "Everyone's downstairs . . . Michael, you know the way."

Could she have said that for my benefit, just to let me know that Michael had been there before?

It was a big party—maybe thirty or forty kids —and as soon as the cast arrived everyone surrounded them, offering congratulations. Michael gave Artie a couple of friendly slugs, then bent down and whispered something to him, and Artie smiled, nodded and said, "Thanks, buddy."

Elizabeth's father took movies of us for the next half hour. Artie really hammed it up. Michael kissed Elizabeth on the side of her face and said, "The part was made for you . . . you were great." And Elizabeth answered, "I'm glad you thought so."

I walked away with a sinking feeling in my stomach. Sybil was standing in the corner talking to some boy. I went over to her and said, "I enjoyed the play a lot . . . you were good."

Sybil laughed. "Thanks, but I know better . . . She introduced me to the boy who turned out to be Elizabeth's younger brother. I wondered if he would make her list.

Erica took me aside, looked in Artie's direction, and said, "He's flying very high . . . I wouldn't be surprised if tonight's the night . . ."

"Good luck," I said, without enthusiasm.

"Oh, here you are." Michael stood next to me and reached for my hand.

"Have we met?" I asked, pulling away.

"What's that supposed to mean?"

"Nothing," I said. "Just forget it." I made my way over to Artie, who was sitting on the couch surrounded by fans. When I got a chance I said, "I know you've heard this all night but you were really sensational."

"Thanks, Kath." He moved over, making room for me beside him.

"How'd you do it? You actually convinced me you were blind."

"I don't know . . . it just comes naturally."

"Seriously, Artie . . ."

"I'm serious. I don't know how I do it. I've always wanted to act . . . ever since I can remember."

"You mean for real . . . professionally?"

"Yeah . . . it's tough to get started but I'm going to give it a try."

"I think you're going to make it."

"I hope you're right . . . where's my buddy?"

"Over there . . . talking to Erica . . ."

"Hey . . ." Artie called, motioning for Michael and Erica to join us.

This time Michael didn't reach for my hand.

I watched and waited all night for some secret look to pass between Elizabeth and Michael but as far as I could tell nothing happened and when we finally got around to talking she was just plain friendly and even said that she remembered me from New Year's Eve, which only made me feel worse.

The party was still going strong when Michael said, "Let's get out of here."

"Why . . . aren't you having a good time?" I asked.

"Not especially . . . are you?"

I didn't answer. I went upstairs to get my

coat and sulked all the way home. Michael didn't say a word. He didn't even look my way.

When we got to my house I unlocked the front door. "Are you coming in?" I asked him.

"Do you want me to?"

"If you want," I said, like it really didn't matter.

"It's up to you," he answered.

"Don't do me any favors." As if I hadn't been waiting all night to be alone with him. I stepped into the foyer.

Michael followed me. We took off our coats. "Did I do something . . . is that it?" he finally asked.

"No."

"Then what?"

"Oh, I don't know . . . just everything . . . thinking about you and Elizabeth . . ."

"You're jealous?" he asked.

"Maybe that's it . . . I'm not sure."

"That's why you've been such a bitch all night?"

"I guess."

He started to laugh. "I didn't know you were the jealous type."

"I'm not!" But as soon as I said it I realized how dumb it sounded and I laughed too.

"Hey . . . I dreamed about you last night," Michael said.

"What was I like?"

"Very sexy . . ."

I took his hand and we went into the den. "I'm sorry I was such an ass tonight."

"Forget it," he said. "It's nice to know you care. Just promise me one thing . . ."

"What?"

"From now on we're honest with each other. If something's bothering you, say it, and I'll do the same . . . agreed?"

"Agreed."

"Good."

We lay down on our rug and after a while, when Michael reached under my skirt I didn't stop him, not then and not when his hand was inside my underpants.

"I want you so much," he said.

"I want you too," I told him, "but I can't . . . I'm not ready, Michael . . ."

"Yes, you are . . . you are . . . I can feel how ready you are."

"No . . ." I pushed his hand away and sat up. "I'm talking about mentally ready."

"Mentally ready," Michael repeated.

"Yes."

"How does a person get mentally ready?" he asked.

"A person has to think . . . a person has to be sure . . ."

"But your body says you want to . . ."

"I have to control my body with my mind."

"Oh, shit . . ." Michael said.

"It's not easy for me either."

"I know . . . I know . . ." He put his arm around me. "Look . . . we can satisfy each other without the whole thing . . ."

"We will . . . soon . . ."

"If I didn't know better I'd think you were a tease."

"I'd never tease you."

"Yeah . . . I know that too."

"You want me to be honest, right?"

"Uh huh."

"Well . . . the thing is . . . I don't know exactly how to do it . . . satisfy you, I mean."

"It's the easiest thing in the world," Michael said, loosening his belt.

"Not now . . ." I told him.

"When?"

"Soon, but not tonight."

"Promises . . . promises . . ."

After Michael went home and I was in bed, trying to fall asleep, I thought about making love with him—the whole thing, like he said. Would I make noises like my mother? I can always tell when my parents are making love because they shut their bedroom door after they think Jamie and I are asleep. It's hard not to listen. My room is right next to theirs. Sometimes I'll hear them laughing softly and other times my mother will let out these little moans or call *Roger . . . Roger . . .* Even though I know it's natural and I'm glad my parents love each other I can't help feeling embarrassed. What would it be like to be in bed with Michael? Sometimes I want to so much—but other times I'm afraid.

7

❦❦

"Guess where we're going over Washington's Birthday?" Michael asked.

I shifted the phone to my other ear. "I give up."

"Skiing."

"But I don't know how."

"I'm going to teach you."

"Really?"

"Yeah . . . we're going to my sister's place in Vermont . . . she'll be calling in a little while to fill your mother in on the details."

"You're serious?"

"You better believe it. Listen, you'll like Sharon, and her husband, Ike, is okay too."

"It sounds great."

"It will be . . . and Kath, wait till you see the snow."

When I hung up I ran into the living room. "Guess where Michael's invited me?"

"To his prom?" Dad asked.

"No . . . nothing like that."

"Well, tell us," Mom said.

"To Vermont . . . to go skiing . . . his sister's got a place there. She's going to call you."

My mother looked at my father.

"I can go, can't I?" I said.

"Well . . ." Dad began.

"Please!"

"You can't expect us to say *yes* just like that, Kath," Mom said.

"We'll have to think about it," Dad told me. "After we hear the details."

Later, when the phone rang, I said, "That must be Michael's sister . . . her name's Sharon."

"I'll take it upstairs," Mom said, but by then Jamie had already answered and was calling, "Hey, Mom . . . telephone . . . somebody named Sharon something."

"What'd she say?" I asked when my mother came back downstairs. "Did you tell her I can go?"

"She sounded very nice," Mom said.

"Go on . . ."

"She said she and her husband would drive you up to Vermont on Friday. It's about a seven hour trip. Their place is near Stowe."

"When would they come home?" Dad asked.

"Monday afternoon."

"That's three nights."

"What's the difference?" I said.

"They have plenty of room, Roger," Mom told him, and I knew then that she was on my side—that she would let me go. "They share the house with two other couples but they'll have it all to themselves over the weekend. She said there are three bedrooms."

"I don't know," my father said.

"Her husband's a resident in internal medicine," Mom said.

"So you won't have to worry about me getting sick," I told my father.

"Just breaking a leg or two," Dad said.

"I'll be very careful . . . I promise."

"I don't know . . . skiiing is a dangerous sport."

"No more dangerous than riding in a car," I argued.

"Give us a chance to talk about it tonight," my father said. "And we'll let you know tomorrow."

"I don't see what there is to discuss . . . it's all very simple."

"I don't like making hasty decisions."

"Mom . . ."

"Dad's right. Let us sleep on it, Kath."

"I want to go very much."

"We know," they both said together.

I don't know how I got through the next day. Talking to Erica helped some. "My mother will let me go but my father seemed kind of scared to say yes."

"That's logical," Erica said. "Fathers have complexes about their little girls. They can't stand the thought of their precious darlings having sex."

"You think that's what's bothering him?"

"Absolutely. It has nothing to do with breaking your leg, like he said . . . it has to do with breaking your cherry."

"Oh, Erica!"

She laughed. "But I'm willing to bet your mother talks him into letting you go."

"God . . . I hope so."

"I'd love to go away with Artie."

"I take it things have improved between the two of you."

"That depends on what you mean by *improved*."

"You know what I mean."

"They haven't improved that way . . . but at least we're getting honest with each other . . . and you can't have a decent relationship without honesty."

"That's just what we were talking about the other night . . . Michael said practically the same thing."

"It's true."

"Yes . . . but you said you were going to do something drastic if nothing happened after the play."

"I did . . . when he took me home from the party and kissed me goodnight on the cheek I came right out and asked him, *Artie, are you queer?*"

"You didn't!"

"Want to bet . . ."

"What'd he say?"

"He said, *I don't know, Erica, but I'm trying to find out.*"

"Jesus . . ."

"So I asked him, *Artie . . . how can you find out when all we ever do is play games . . . Monopoly, bingo, chess, backgammon . . . they're coming out of my ears.*"

"And?"

"He said, *I'm scared to try, Erica.* Now that's being honest, wouldn't you say?"

"Definitely."

"So I told him not to worry . . . that I'll help him find out and he said he'd really appreciate that. So next weekend, while you're in Vermont . . ."

"If I get to go," I said.

"If you get to go . . . Artie and I will be trying to get at the truth."

After school I walked over to the library. "It's okay," my mother said, before I could ask. "The stores are open late tonight and when I passed the *Sports Center* at lunchtime I noticed this terrific looking ski jacket in your size . . . reduced ten dollars."

"I really can go?"

"Why else would you need a ski jacket?" Mom asked.

"Oh Mom!" I hugged her as hard as I could.

"You're the greatest . . . you're the best mother that ever was!"

"Remember that the next time we disagree."

Later that night, when Mom and I came home from shopping, I modeled my new ski clothes for Jamie and Dad. My jacket is yellow, red and blue and I bought navy ski pants and a hat to match out of my savings.

"At least it's bright enough for them to find you if you're buried in an avalanche," my father said.

"How can I get buried in an avalanche with Michael watching out for me?"

"They don't have avalanches in Vermont, anyway," Jamie said. "I wish I could go too."

"Not this time," I told her.

"I'd do all the cooking."

"Sorry, Jamie."

"Michael loves my cooking."

"No way."

"Drats!"

When Michael called I told him it was all set. "I even got ski clothes."

"You didn't have to go out and buy anything. Sharon was going to lend you a parka and warm-ups."

"Well . . . now she won't have to . . ."

"Yeah . . . but you'll still have to rent your boots and skis."

"I know . . . don't worry about it . . ."

"Your lift ticket's on me, though."

"Okay, if you insist . . . and Michael . . ."

"Yeah?"

"I can't wait until Friday."

"That makes two of us."

Before I went to sleep my father came into my room and sat down on the edge of my bed, like he used to do when I was little. He took my hand.

"I'm glad you decided I could go to Vermont, Dad."

"Well . . . you'll be off to college in the fall . . . I have to let you go sooner or later . . . I guess you're not a little girl anymore."

"I guess not."

"You have a lot of common sense, Kath. You've always made intelligent decisions . . . still, you and Michael are very young."

"We're not planning to elope, if that's what you're worried about."

"I'm not worried. I just don't want to see you get hurt."

"I told you, I'll be careful."

"Not that kind of hurt, Kath."

"Oh Dad . . ."

"I like Michael . . . and it's not that I don't trust him . . ."

"Daddy . . . he's not a sex fiend . . . so please stop worrying about us."

"I can't help it."

I sat up and hugged him. "Everything's going to be fine . . . really."

8

As soon as we got to the ski house Michael jumped out of the car and bombarded me with snowballs. There was beautiful fresh snow everywhere and miles and miles of woods, with icicles hanging from every tree. I ran from him, half-laughing and half-screaming, but he didn't listen until Ike grabbed him by the arm and said, "Work now . . . play later." He led Michael back to the car, opened the trunk and pointed to all the stuff that had to be lugged inside.

I helped Sharon unpack the groceries. She was tall and thin, like Michael, with the same color hair, but the shape of her eyes made her look like she was squinting, even when she wasn't. Ike was shorter than Sharon but very broad, with practically no neck. He had a bald spot on the top of his head. I wondered if it will grow until he's totally bald and if it does, will Sharon care? How would I feel if Michael was bald? I'm not sure. I love his hair—the color, the way it feels, the smell of it. I'd be disappointed if it all fell out.

After everything was put away in the kitchen I explored the house. There was one big room with a gray stone fireplace, a beat-up shaggy rug, and a bunch of pillows scattered on the floor. The kitchen opened right into it. Then there was Ike and Sharon's bedroom. They had a private bath. Upstairs there were two more bedrooms, connected by another bathroom, which meant that Michael and I would be sharing. I was glad I'd been honest with him when he picked me up that afternoon. I'd led him into the kitchen while my mother was talking with Sharon and Ike in the living room.

"I have something to tell you," I said.

"Go ahead."

"I got my period this morning."

"Oh."

"A week early."

"Oh."

"My mother says it probably happened because I was so excited . . . about going away and all . . . I just thought you should know."

"You're right."

"In case I have to make some stops on the drive up . . ."

"You don't feel sick or anything, do you?"

"No, I'm fine . . . just disappointed . . . I hope you're not."

"Hell, no . . . why should I be disappointed as

long as you can still come with us," he'd said, taking my hand.

When Michael and Ike had finished unloading the car and we were all unpacked, the four of us sat around the fire, sipping mugs of steaming coffee laced with brandy. Sharon told me all about her job. She's an anthropologist, working for the Museum of Natural History, but she hopes to go on a field trip soon, maybe this summer. When I heard that I asked her if she'd be a speaker at our Career Day program in April, because most kids don't get to meet anthropologists every day. Sharon said she'd like that a lot. My guidance counselor, Mrs. Handelsman, will be pleased since she's having trouble finding enough interesting speakers, especially young women.

We were all tired from the trip and when Sharon started yawning the rest of us joined her. "Let's hit the sack," Ike said, and he and Sharon said goodnight and went to their room.

Michael and I looked at each other.

"You can use the bathroom first," he told me.

"Okay."

We went upstairs. "I'll wake you at 7:30 so we can get an early start."

"Okay . . . fine."

He kissed me on the cheek. "Just yell when you're done in the bathroom."

"I will."

"Well . . . goodnight."

"Goodnight . . ." I put my forehead against his chest. "You're sure you're not mad?"

"No . . . come on, Kath . . . it's okay. Get a good night's sleep and I'll see you in the morning."

I nodded, then went to my room while Michael went to his. I felt like crying. Our goodnight hadn't been at all the way I'd wanted it. I put on my long white nightgown. It's the prettiest one I own, made out of soft brushed nylon, with angel sleeves and tiny buttons shaped like hearts. I was hoping Michael would see me in it.

I used the bathroom, called, "Finished . . ." and got into bed. I listened as Michael ran the water and flushed the toilet. When it was quiet I called out again. "Goodnight, Michael . . ."

"Kath . . ."

"Yes?"

"Can I come in for a second?"

"Sure." I sat up in bed and hugged the covers to me.

Michael was wearing baggy blue pajamas. He sat down on the bed and I put my arms around him and a funny sound came out of his throat and we kissed.

"Your sister . . ." I muttered, when we came up for a breath.

"Don't worry."

We kissed again. Then Michael held me away and said, "I wasn't going to touch you tonight . . . just to prove I didn't get you up here for sex."

"I'd have been disappointed," I told him. "I even wore my best nightgown. Do you like it?"

"It covers too much of you but it's nice and soft." Michael reached over and turned out the lamp on the night table. "How do you work these crazy buttons?" he asked, trying to undo my nightgown.

I unbuttoned them myself.

"I want to feel you against me," Michael said and he took off the top of his pajamas. Then he lay down and put his arms around me.

"Oh . . . it feels nice this way," I whispered, as my hands wandered across his naked shoulders and down his back.

Michael kissed me and reached down between my legs but I caught his hand and moved it away. "No . . . not tonight . . ."

"I don't care."

"But I do." It wasn't so much that I didn't want him to touch me, because I did—it was just that I didn't think it was a good idea for either one of us to get carried away. "Michael . . . don't get too worked up . . . okay . . ."

"I'm already worked up."

He didn't have to tell me.

We kissed one more time and then he touched my face gently and said, "I love you, Katherine. I really mean it . . . I love you."

I could have said it back to him right away. I was thinking it all along. I was thinking, *I love you, Michael.* But can you really love someone you've seen just nineteen times in your life?

"I've never said that before," he told me.

"I'm glad."

"I want to hold you all night."

"I want you to."

We slept with our arms around each other till Ike's voice woke us in the morning.

9

It was a sunny cold day, but not windy. Michael said it was perfect for skiing. I got dressed in my long underwear, turtleneck shirt, ski pants, sweater, two pairs of socks and snow boots. I could hardly move.

Sharon was still asleep but Ike had breakfast on the table—cereal, eggs and buns. "No raisins," Michael said, passing the plate to me.

"How'd you know I don't like raisins?"

"New Year's Day . . . remember?"

"Oh, that . . ." I said, picturing myself at Sybil's table, picking raisins out of a bun. "You have a good memory."

"For some things," Michael said and he smiled.

After breakfast Ike gave Michael the car keys and told him to drive me into town to rent my equipment. "Their prices are better than at the lodge. With a little luck Sharon should be ready to go when you get back."

We went to the Alpine Ski Shop. When Michael was finally satisfied that I had the right size boots he showed me how to work the buckles and also how to walk in them without killing myself, which wasn't easy.

Sharon was dressed and ready to go when we got back to the house. From there it was just a short ride to the slopes. They had season tickets and Michael bought mine. When I saw the prices I said, "I never knew skiing was such an expensive sport."

"That's its only drawback," Michael told me.

"Let's go to the Ladies' Room before we get our skis on," Sharon said. "It's such a pain to have to come in before lunch."

I followed her into the lodge and downstairs. We both used the toilets. While we were washing our hands Sharon said that the reason so many beginners get hurt is because they try to learn to ski themselves. "I just want you to know that Michael is a qualified instructor . . . otherwise Ike and I would insist that you take class lessons."

"He's really that good?"

"Just wait till you see him in action."

I smiled. Sharon caught on and laughed. "I meant skiing action," she said.

"I know it."

"My brother's a very nice boy, isn't he?"

"I think so."

"But he seems so . . . well . . . vulnerable."

"How do you mean?"

"Oh . . . he's so open . . . I wouldn't want to see him get hurt."

She didn't look at me when she said that. She looked into the mirror and rubbed some kind of ointment on her lips. I didn't know what to say to her after that. Did she think Michael would get hurt because of me? Did she think I was just using him or what?

"Well . . . let's get going." Sharon put the tube of ointment into her pocket. "And Katherine . . ."

"Yes?"

"I'm sorry if I sounded like a mother hen just now . . . I've really got to stop worrying about Michael. After all, he's all grown up, isn't he?"

"Yes," I said, "he is." It's funny that Sharon worries about Michael in the same way that my father worries about me.

We went upstairs, found Michael and Ike waiting outside, and arranged to meet at the lodge at noon. Sharon and Ike went off to ski the more difficult slopes.

Michael got me onto my skis. They were very short and hardly stuck out at all behind me. He said it's much easier to learn with the short kind and as I improve I'll get longer ones. I didn't think that would be likely.

"First one foot and then the other," Michael said, as I tried to walk. But I got tangled up and tripped over myself. Both of us were laugh-

ing by then. "Let the ski slide across the snow
.. don't try to raise it."

"Oh . . . like this?" I asked.

"Very good," he said, taking my arm.

Somehow we made it to the chairlift. "Just
grab the side and sit down when the lift comes,"
Michael told me. "Ready . . . now!" I sat down
and was surprised that I landed in the chair
and that Michael was right beside me. Before
I had a chance to think about it we were going
up.

Michael pulled the safety bar down, looked at
me and said, "You're going to love it."

I nodded and tried to smile back.

"We're getting off at the beginners' slope so
you don't have to worry."

"I'm not worried."

"You look scared to death."

"Don't be silly . . . I can't wait to learn to ski."
But I was thinking, we're going up so high . . .
how will I ever get down? My father was
right . . . I am going to break a leg . . . I'm going
to fall off this chairlift and break a leg . . .
maybe even two . . . probably two legs and an
arm . . . possibly more than that even.

"Getting off is tricky," Michael said and he
flipped the safety bar up, leaving me free to
fall off in mid-air. "Just do what I do . . . point
your skis up."

I did what he said.

"That's it . . . now get ready . . . we're going
to stand up in a minute and then just let the

lift push you away . . . got it?" Michael grabbed me but I forgot everything he'd said and he had to push me out of the way or the lift would have whacked me in the head and naturally when he pushed me like that I fell over.

"Damn!"

Michael laughed.

"It's not funny."

"You better get used to it. You're going to be on the ground a lot today, but cheer up . . . tomorrow you'll be an expert."

"Ha!"

He helped me to my feet. My nose was running. "Here . . ." he said, pulling a tissue out of his pocket.

I blew my nose.

"I forgot to tell you . . . everybody's nose runs when they ski."

"Swell."

"Ready?"

"Are you sure I'm going to be able to do this?"

"Didn't you tell me how coordinated you are . . . a tennis whiz . . . a modern dance freak . . ."

"I never said *whiz* and I certainly never said *freak!*"

"Relax . . . anybody can learn to ski."

"I hope so. Just one simple question before we start, okay?"

"Sure . . . go ahead."

"How am I going to get down the mountain?"

"You're going to ski down, Kath."

"I was afraid you'd say that."

Michael was right. I spent more time on the ground than on my feet on my first try. But by noon I'd been up and down the beginners' slope three times. On my third try I didn't even fall when I got off the chairlift and if I wasn't skiing exactly, well, at least I was doing something.

Sharon and Ike were already at the lodge, saving a table for lunch. "Hey . . . how'd it go?" Ike asked.

"You wouldn't believe how good she's doing," Michael told them. "I'm really proud of her!"

"Did you enjoy it?" Sharon asked.

"Yes, it's fun . . . it's a very good feeling."

"Invigorating," Ike said.

"That's it . . . invigorating."

"And it builds up a good appetite," Sharon said. "I'm starving . . ."

"Let's get on line," Michael said. "I don't want to waste a lot of time in here . . . I want to get Kath back on the slopes."

After lunch we tried a different trail. "Skis together," Michael said, "let them run across the slope . . . glide . . . glide . . . good . . . okay . . . now, kick your heels down the mountain . . . that's it . . . great . . ."

"I did it," I called. "I actually stopped!"

"Yeah . . . now you won't have to sit down every time you lose your balance."

I scooped up some snow and threw it at him, but he ducked and laughed.

We skied until 4:00, when the lifts closed.

"I've had the best time," I told Michael as he helped me out of my bindings. "I really loved it."

"I'm glad," he said. "You're not a bad student either . . . considering."

"Considering what?"

"Oh, just considering." He kissed me on the nose.

I had no idea how sore my muscles were until we got back to the house. Michael had to pull me out of the car. "I hurt all over," I said. "My legs don't want to hold me up."

"A bath will help," Sharon told me. "Soak a long time and keep adding hot water . . . there's plenty of time for a nap too. We don't eat until seven."

I bathed, then fell asleep and didn't wake up until Michael whispered in my ear. "Kath . . . time for dinner . . ."

"Mmmmm . . ." I rolled over.

He sat on the edge of the bed. "You need some help getting up?"

"Mmmmm . . ." I opened my eyes. His face was next to mine.

"Hi," he said.

"Hi . . ." I pulled him down and held him close.

"Later . . . it's time to get up now."

"No . . . not yet."

"I'll have to help you if you can't do it yourself . . ."

"Mmmmm . . . soon . . ."

Michael got off the bed and I closed my eyes again. I heard the water running in the bathroom. Then he was back, standing over me, calling, "Kath . . ." and when I opened my eyes he was holding a glass of water over my head, threatening.

"You wouldn't . . . " I cried, jumping out of bed.

"Now that you're up I won't have to," he told me, "but next time you don't get a second chance."

After dinner we sat around the fire and talked for a while, then Michael got up and went to the window. "The stars are out," he said. "You want to take a walk?" My insides still turn over when he looks at me that certain way.

I got my boots and jacket.

"Don't get frostbitten," Sharon called after us.

As soon as we were outside and away from the house we kissed. "I had to get out of there," Michael told me. "All I could think about was being alone with you."

"I know," I said, ". . . same here."

We held hands as we walked. "I've never seen so many stars," I said.

"That's because it's so dark and clear . . . no city lights, no traffic, no pollution . . ."

"I love to look at stars."

"I love to look at you."

"Oh, Michael . . . come on . . ." I gave him a friendly punch.

When we got back to the house Sharon and Ike were stretched out in front of the fire smoking grass. "Hi," Sharon said. "Did you freeze your tails off?"

"Almost," I told her. I was really surprised to see Sharon smoking. I thought she was so straight, especially after that business about Michael being vulnerable and getting hurt.

"Your cheeks are bright red," Ike told me.

"They always get that way."

"I like them," Michael said, putting his hand against my face.

Ike held the joint to his lips and took a long drag. Then he offered it to Michael.

"You want to?" Michael asked me.

"I don't think so," I said.

"We'll skip it," Michael told Ike, taking my hand. "Katherine's very tired."

"Goodnight," I said, as Michael and I headed upstairs.

"Get a good night's sleep," Sharon called.

"We will."

Michael lay down on the bed in my room.

"I thought you don't smoke," I said.

"I don't, anymore . . . except with them, sometimes . . ."

"Oh." I walked over to the window and opened it a little. I like plenty of fresh air in my bedroom. "I've only tried once . . . and nothing good happened . . . I felt sick to my stomach."

"It can be like that the first time."

"Besides," I said, going to the dresser and picking up my hairbrush, "I don't like to lose control of myself." I was thinking about later, wondering if he would get into bed with me again. Last night was so nice.

"I know it," Michael said.

"Would I . . . if I smoked again?"

"I don't know . . . probably not."

I started brushing my hair. Michael was watching me. I wanted to ask him *what next?* Did he have plans? Did he already know? I wished I had a script to follow so I wouldn't make any mistakes. *Don't forget about my period, Michael,* I felt like saying. "There are kids at school who are high all the time."

"That's different," he said.

"I suppose . . ." I put my brush down. "I'm surprised that Sharon and Ike smoke at all . . . I mean, Ike being a doctor and all." I opened the dresser drawer and pulled out my night-gown. I should wear it, shouldn't I? Yes, but leave it unbuttoned this time.

"They're not exactly addicts," Michael said.

"I know that . . . should I use the bathroom first?"

"Sure."

I put on my nightgown and bikini under-pants and after I'd washed and brushed my teeth I said, "You can use the bathroom now."

I got into bed and waited. In a few minutes Michael opened my door. He was wearing his same blue pajamas. He kind of waved at me and said, "Hi."

"Hi," I answered.

He put his glasses on the night table, turned out the light and climbed into bed beside me. After we'd kissed for awhile he took off his pajama top, then said, "Let's take yours off too . . . it's in the way."

I slipped my nightgown over my head and dropped it to the floor. Then there were just my bikini pants and Michael's pajama bottoms between us. We kissed again. Feeling him against me that way made me so excited I couldn't lie still. He rolled over on top of me and we moved together again and again and it felt so good I didn't ever want to stop—until I came.

After a minute I reached for Michael's hand. "Show me what to do," I said.

"Do whatever you want."

"Help me, Michael . . . I feel so stupid."

"Don't," he said, wiggling out of his pajama bottoms. He led my hand to his penis. "Katherine . . . I'd like you to meet Ralph . . . Ralph, this is Katherine. She's a very good friend of mine."

"Does every penis have a name?"

"I can only speak for my own."

In books penises are always described as hot and throbbing but Ralph felt like ordinary skin. Just his shape was different—that and the fact that he wasn't smooth, exactly—as if there was a lot going on under the skin. I don't know why I'd been so nervous about touching Michael. Once I got over being scared I let my hands go everywhere. I wanted to feel every part of him.

While I was experimenting, I asked, "Is this right?"

And Michael whispered, "Everything's right."

When I kissed his face it was all sweaty and his eyes were half-closed. He took my hand and led it back to Ralph, showing me how to hold him, moving my hand up and down according to his rhythm. Soon Michael moaned and I felt him come—a pulsating feeling, a throbbing, like the books said—then wetness. Some of it got on my hand but I didn't let go of Ralph.

We were both quiet for a while, then Michael reached for the tissue box by the side of the bed. He passed it to me. "Here . . . I didn't mean to get you."

"That's all right . . . I don't mind . . ." I pulled out some tissues.

He took the box back. "I'm glad," he said, wiping up his stomach.

I kissed the mole on the side of his face. "Did I do okay . . . considering my lack of experience?"

He laughed, then put his arms around me. "You did just fine . . . Ralph liked it a lot."

I settled next to Michael with my head on his chest.

"Kath . . ."

"Hmmmm?"

"Remember last night when I said I loved you?"

"Yes."

"Well . . . I really meant it . . . it's not just the sex thing . . . that's part of it . . . but it's more than that . . . you know?"

"I know . . . because I love you too," I whispered into his chest. Saying it the first time was the hardest. There's something so final about it. The second time I sat up and said it right to him. "I love you, Michael Wagner."

"Forever?" he asked.

"Forever," I said.

10

"Do you still like each other?" Jamie said, as soon as I got back from Vermont. She and Mom and Dad were waiting up for me in the den. I collapsed on the sofa. Seven hours in a Volkswagen is a long time.

"Well, of course we do . . . why shouldn't we?"

"Daddy said sometimes spending a lot of time together can end a romance faster than anything else."

My father actually blushed when I looked at him. "Were you hoping this would end it?" I asked.

"Don't be silly, Kath," Dad said.

"Then why would you have said such a thing?"

"It was a general discussion . . . not one about you and Michael."

"We also discussed how being together can make a romance even stronger," my mother said, to rescue my father, I think.

"Well, that's more like it!" I said, looking at Dad. "Being together made ours stronger."

"I'm glad," Jamie said.

When I got into bed, half an hour later, my father came to my room. "You think I don't approve of you and Michael . . ." he began.

"Do you?"

"Of course I do. I'm just afraid you'll get too involved . . . that's all."

"What's wrong with being involved?"

"Maybe that's the wrong word. What I mean is, I don't want to see you tied down."

"Who's tied down?"

My father sighed. "Will you stop throwing questions back at me . . . what I'm trying to say is, you're too young to make lifetime decisions."

"I'm not making lifetime decisions."

"You have to consider the future, Kath."

"What about it?"

"There you go again."

"I'm sorry," I said, ". . . but the future will take care of itself."

The next morning I waited until my father had gone off to his tennis game and Jamie left for school. Then I caught my mother on her way into the shower and asked, "Does Daddy want me to stop seeing Michael?"

"Of course not."

"Because I won't . . . not even if he asks me to . . ."

"He's not going to ask you . . . he'd just like

to see you get around more with other people . . . the way you used to . . ."

"But I don't want to . . . I don't want to be
with any other boy."

"I understand, Kath . . . and deep down inside, so does Dad . . . he's just having trouble
accepting it . . ."

"I can tell."

"Say, aren't you going to be late for school?"

"So I'll miss first period study hall . . . big
deal!"

"If you want I'll drive you over as soon as
I'm dressed."

"Okay."

I got my books together and found my clean
gymsuit in the laundry room. Then I went out
to the garage and started the car. I've had my
license since September but I hardly ever get
any driving practice.

Mom came out of the house pulling on her
hat and gloves. She wears the same kind of
white knitted hat that I do only she doesn't pull
it over her forehead the right way. She shoves
it back on her head because she says it makes
her face itch.

"Brrr . . . it's cold out!" Mom opened the car
door.

"Want me to drive?" I asked.

"No . . . the side streets are still icy."

I slid over and my mother got in behind the
wheel.

On the way to school I said, "Mom . . . *were* you a virgin when you got married?"

My mother kept looking straight ahead but she tightened her grip on the wheel.

I quickly added, "I mean, I know you said you were, but . . ."

We stopped at a red light. Mom turned to me. "I was a virgin until we were engaged . . . not married."

"How about Dad . . ."

"There were double standards then . . . boys were supposed to get plenty of experience before marriage."

The car behind us tooted. "The light's green," I said.

"Oh . . . " We drove up East Broad Street and under the railroad tracks.

"Are you glad you waited?" I asked.

"I don't think of it in terms of waiting . . . I was just twenty."

"If you had it to do over again, would you still wait until you were engaged?"

"Everything's different now. I wouldn't have married so young in the first place."

"But would you have waited?"

"I can't answer that . . . I just don't know."

I didn't say anything more but when we got to school instead of just dropping me off my mother pulled into the lot and turned off the ignition. "Look, Kath . . ." she said, "I've always been honest with you about sex . . ."

"I know."

"But you have to be sure you can handle the situation before you jump into it . . . sex is a commitment . . . once you're there you can't go back to holding hands."

"I know it."

"And when you give yourself both mentally and physically . . . well, you're completely vulnerable."

"I've heard that before."

"It's true," my mother said. "It's up to you to decide what's right and what's wrong . . . I'm not going to tell you to go ahead but I'm not going to forbid it either. It's too late for any of that. I expect you to handle it with a sense of responsibility though . . . either way."

"I wasn't asking for personal reasons, Mom . . . I was just curious, really . . ."

"Of course . . . " She reached out and touched my face. "Well . . . have a good day."

We looked at each other for a minute and then I did something I haven't done in a while. I leaned over and kissed my mother.

"I absolutely can't believe it," Erica said, after I'd told her about my weekend. "You're still a virgin!"

"I'm not saying one way or the other."

"But I can tell."

"How?"

"I just can . . . I'd know in a second if you weren't."

We were in the cafeteria, at our usual table

and Erica was eating a hotdog, the lunch special of the day. I am probably the only living American who doesn't like hotdogs so I had a cheese sandwich on my tray—that and a package of Oreos. "Look," I said, "what I do with Michael is private ... it's not something I want to talk about ..."

Erica gave me a hurt look. "Sure ... okay ..."

"Try to understand, Erica ..."

"I do ... I do ..."

"When you're in love you want to keep it to yourself ... that's all I'm saying."

"So you really do love him?"

"Yes."

"And he loves you?"

"Yes."

"He actually came right out and told you?"

"Uh huh."

"God ... that's romantic!"

"I thought you don't believe in romance."

"I don't," Erica said, slurping up the end of her milk.

We carried our trays to the side table. "Don't you want to know about me and Artie?" Erica asked.

"Well, sure ... but I don't want to pry."

"We played strip poker on Saturday night."

"You didn't!"

Erica laughed. "Right down to our birthday suits."

"Suppose your parents had walked in?"

"They respect my privacy."

"So do mine . . . but still . . ."

"Anyway, we didn't do a thing but touch. I'm beginning to feel like a therapist."

"You could be doing him more harm than good."

"I've thought about that . . . but he's very open about his problem. He's not gay . . . we've determined that. He's just impotent. I've been reading up on it and I'm almost sure I can help him."

"But Erica . . . if you want to get laid so badly why don't you find somebody else?"

"I could get laid tomorrow," she said, "but that's not the point anymore. I want to make it with Artie."

"Why?"

"Because I think I can help him, for one thing, and because . . . well, just because."

"I don't know . . . it still sounds to me like you'd both be better off if you'd just forget it."

"No chance . . . we really like each other . . . even though it's nothing like you and Michael . . . not everybody can be so lucky . . ."

11

Usually March is a slow month. There aren't any school holidays, the weather is still cold and dreary, the teachers get after you to work harder, and I can't believe that it will ever be spring.

This March was different. I felt on top of the world. Michael and I saw each other whenever we could. We went skiing at Great Gorge, twice, and one Sunday we went to Madison Square Garden to a Rangers' game with Erica and Artie. The Rangers lost and Artie took it very hard, as if he'd been personally responsible or something. I tried to cheer him up on our way out of the Garden. "Win some . . . lose some . . ." I said.

Artie shook his head.

"Look . . . it was just a game."

"Nothing is *just* a game."

"So they'll win next time."

"Next time isn't good enough."

We walked to a Beef & Brew and were seated

in a booth. While we were waiting to give our orders Erica said, "Did you know Artie's been accepted at the American Academy of Dramatic Arts?"

"Hey . . . that's great," I said. "You're really on your way now . . ."

"On my way nowhere . . ." Artie said. "My old man won't let me go."

Erica turned to him. "You didn't tell me that . . ."

"Yeah . . .well . . . he just made up his mind. It's a four year college or nothing."

"He can't do that," Erica said.

"No . . . who do you think's paying the tuition?"

"Listen . . ." I said, "you can major in drama anyway."

"The eternal optimist speaks again," Artie said.

"I'm sorry . . . I was just trying to look on the bright side of things." I glanced over at Michael, hoping he would come to my rescue but he didn't say anything. I guess he knew about Artie's father already.

"You've got to stand up for your rights!" Erica said. "Refuse to go anywhere but the American Academy . . ."

"Lay off!" Michael said, suddenly, and something in his voice made Erica stop.

All four of us studied our menus then, or pretended to, and the silence in our booth was uncomfortable. Finally the waitress came along and said, "Okay . . . what'll it be?"

Later, when Michael and I were at my house, alone, I said, "I've never seen Artie that way . . . he was so depressed."

"I know."

"Usually he's all fun and games."

"That's his public image."

"Is the private Artie different?"

"Just sometimes . . ."

"Did you hear him jump on everything I said?"

"I heard . . . but I've seen him that way before. He'll be okay in a couple of days. You've got to understand how he feels about school . . . he really hates it. I don't think he'll make it through one year of college, let alone four . . ."

"I didn't know . . ."

"It wasn't your fault."

"Do you think he and Erica are good for each other?"

"That's not my business . . . besides, every girl at school has the hots for him since the play and he's not interested . . . that must prove something."

"Would you be . . . interested . . ."

"Oh, sure. I only go with you because I can't get anything better." He pulled me down next to him. "We can't do anything to help Artie, right now."

"I suppose not . . ."

"We can help Ralph, though," he said, moving my hand to his belt buckle.

On Thursday Michael called to say that Sharon and Ike were taking some time off to go skiing and they'd asked him to join them and his parents said, yes, he could miss a week of school, because this was a special occasion, and the three of them were leaving the next morning and wouldn't be back until the following Sunday.

"Ten days?" I said. "Two entire weekends?"

"It's very important, Kath . . . I'm working toward my instructor's pin . . . you know that."

"I know . . . I know . . ."

That first weekend my parents didn't leave me alone for a minute. You'd have thought I was a widow. They took me out to dinner on Friday night, and on Saturday Jamie and I went shopping. Then Grandma called and asked me to stay overnight at her apartment so I packed a bag and Mom and Dad drove me into New York.

On Sunday morning Grandpa and I went for a walk in Central Park and that afternoon, Grandma took me to see a revival of *Gone With the Wind,* her all-time favorite picture, which she has seen sixteen times, so far. After it, when she asked me what I thought of Clark Gable, and I told her that his ears stuck out, she shook her head and said, "I'm disappointed in you, Kath." But I knew she was just teasing.

The school week dragged on. Jamie said I looked like a sick dog—well, that's how I felt. At dinner one night my father asked me if I'm going steady with Michael.

"We don't call it *going steady*," I told him. "But we are *going together*."

"Does that mean you can't see anyone else?" he asked.

"That means I don't want to see anyone else."

"I went steady once," Mom said, stirring a teaspoon of honey into her tea. "And I wore his school ring on a chain around my neck. His name was Seymour Mandelbaum."

"Seymour Mandelbaum?" Jamie said and cracked up.

"I was a junior and he was a senior," Mom told us. "I wonder what ever happened to him."

I got the feeling that Mom was talking about her old boyfriend so my father would see that it didn't matter about Michael and me going together.

Then Dad surprised me by saying, "I went steady twice."

"You?" I asked.

"Once when I was in tenth grade . . . I gave her my I.D. bracelet . . . and once when I was a freshman in college."

He and Mom started reminiscing about their college days. I didn't tell them that with Michael and me it's different. That it's not just some fifties fad, like going steady. That with us it is love—real, true honest-to-god love.

The next morning, at breakfast, Dad said, "I still think you'd be happier if you weren't tied down to one boy."

"You don't understand," I explained. "I'm not unhappy. I just miss him."

"What about next year?" Mom asked. "You're going to be apart then."

My mother's question sent me rushing to my guidance counselor first thing. When she saw me she said, "Oh, Katherine . . . I was just working on the final arrangements for Career Day . . . April 25 is just around the corner."

"This isn't about Career Day," I said.

"Then what?"

"I've got to apply to another school . . . right away."

"It's late to apply," she said.

"I know . . . but this is an emergency."

She took my folder out of her files. "Let's see . . ." she said, thumbing through it, "you've applied to Michigan, Penn State and Denver . . . all good schools."

"But I really want to go to University of Vermont . . . either there or Middlebury."

"Why this sudden change?"

"I've got a friend . . . and we want to be together."

"Have you discussed this with your parents?"

"Not yet . . ."

"I'll need their permission and even so . . . I can't promise you anything . . . Middlebury's tough and Vermont takes their own first."

"I'm sure I can get my parents' permission by tomorrow."

But later, when I told Mom, she said, "No!" Just like that. "I don't think that's wise . . . you've already applied to three schools."

"But Mom . . . you know what it's like for me this week . . . being away from him."

"You can see each other on vacations . . . and even weekends now and then . . . and if it's that serious between you it'll grow while you're apart."

"You really believe that?" I asked.

"Yes, Kath . . . I do. And you can always transfer after two years . . . or he can."

"I thought you'd be on my side," I said.

"I am," she told me.

Just when I was feeling really down, knowing that we can't be together next year, and that now I faced another weekend without him, the phone rang. It was Michael.

"I'm home," he said.

"But today's only Friday."

"I know . . . I took the train . . . I got back this morning."

"Wasn't the skiing any good?"

"It was super."

"Then why'd you come back early?"

"Do you really have to ask?"

When I answered the door, two hours later, he took my hand and kind of brushed my cheek with his face.

"Hi," I managed to say.

We went to the 8:00 movie and after it, on the way back to the car, Michael said, "Guess what I have?"

"VD?" I asked, laughing. I expected Michael to crack up over my joke, but he didn't.

"Why'd you say a stupid thing like that?" he said, seriously.

"I don't know . . . it just popped out."

"That means it's in your subconscious."

"It is not! It was just the way you said it . . . you sounded like that commercial where the boy calls the girl and then she calls another boy and he . . ."

"Yeah . . . I've seen it."

"I didn't mean for you to take it personally."

"Well, I did."

"I'm sorry . . ."

"I had it once."

We stopped walking and dropped hands. "You had VD?"

"I got it from this girl in Maine . . . the only time I ever got laid."

"You've only been laid once?"

"Well, twice . . . but with the same girl."

"That's all?"

"What do you mean, *that's all*? What'd you expect?"

"I don't know . . . I thought you had lots of experience."

"Yeah, well . . . the clap turned me off for a while."

"I can imagine," I said. We started walking again, this time without holding hands. "Did you tell the girl in Maine?"

"I couldn't . . . I didn't even know her last name. She was just somebody I met on the beach."

"Oh."

"Look, Kath . . . that was last summer . . . so don't go worrying about it . . . I'm fine now."

"Who said anything about worrying?" I asked, but I must have looked like something was wrong because Michael said, "Then what?"

"You should never take chances."

"That's easy for you to say . . . you always think of everything, don't you?"

"I try to . . ."

We got to the car and Michael unlocked the door. "You probably never took a chance in your life."

"What's that supposed to mean?" I said, sliding into my seat.

"Nothing . . . forget it." He got in, banged his fists against the steering wheel and said, "Oh, shit!"

"What's wrong?" I asked.

He looked straight ahead.

"Can't you at least tell me what's wrong?"

"I don't know . . ." he finally answered. "I've been waiting to be with you all week and now nothing's going right. I'm all tangled up inside."

"Same here." I said.

"Damn . . ." he reached for me. We held each other and then, for some stupid reason I started to cry, which I never do, especially in front of other people.

"Don't, Kath . . . please . . ."

"Same here," I said.

"Look," he said, "let's start over . . . okay?"

I nodded, then took out a tissue and blew my nose.

"Guess what I have?" Michael asked again.

This time I said, "I give up . . . what?"

"The key to my sister's apartment."

"That's what you were trying to tell me before?"

"Uh huh."

I started to laugh. I couldn't help it. The more I thought about it, the funnier it seemed, and the harder I laughed. In a minute Michael was laughing with me. He took my hand. "So . . . you want to go there?" he said.

"I'm not sure."

"We don't have to do anything . . . we can just talk."

12

Sharon and Ike live in a garden apartment in Springfield. All the outside doors are painted green. "I hope nobody thinks we're trying to break in," I said, as Michael put the key in the lock, "because there's an old lady watching us." I pointed to a window.

"Don't worry about her." Michael pushed the door open. "That's Mrs. Cornick . . . she lives downstairs . . . she's always in the window." He waved at her and she dropped her shade. "Come on . . . their place is upstairs."

The stairs led into the living room. "It's nice," I said, looking around. There wasn't much furniture but they had a fantastic Persian rug and three posters of chimpanzees riding bicycles. I walked over to a plant and held up a leaf. "Too much water . . . that's why the edges are turning brown."

"I'll tell Sharon you said so."

"No, don't . . . then she'll know I've been here."

"So?"

"So, I just don't want her to know . . . okay?"

"I don't see why . . . but okay. You want something to eat?"

"Maybe . . ." We went to the kitchen which was small and narrow with no outside window.

Michael opened the refrigerator. "How about an apple . . . or a grapefruit? That's about all I see."

"I'll have an apple."

He polished it off on his shirt, then tossed it to me. "I'll show you around the place," he said.

Since I'd already seen the living room and the kitchen we started with the bathroom. "Notice the indoor plumbing." Michael demonstrated how to flush the toilet.

"Very interesting," I told him.

"And hot and cold running water." He turned on both faucets.

"Luxurious."

"Also, a genuine bathtub." He stepped into it and I pulled the curtain around him. While he was in there I wrapped the apple core in some toilet paper and hid it in my pocketbook. Michael jumped out of the tub, grabbed my hand and said, "Onward . . ."

We both knew there was just one room left to see. "Presenting . . ." Michael said, and he bowed, "the bedroom."

There was a brass bed, covered with a patchwork quilt and a LOVE poster hanging on the wall, above it. There were also two small chests, piled high with books.

Michael jumped up and down on the bed while I watched from the doorway. "Good mattress . . ." he said, "nice and firm . . . in case you're interested."

"For jumping, you mean?"

"For whatever . . ." He lay down and looked at the ceiling. "Kath . . ."

"Hmmm . . ."

"Come here . . ."

"I thought we were just going to talk."

"We are . . . but you're so far away . . . I don't want to shout."

"I can hear you fine."

"Cut it out . . . will you?"

I went to the bed and sat on the edge. "There's one thing I'd really like to know . . ."

"What's that?"

"Have you brought any other girls up here?"

"Your jealous streak is showing."

"I admit it . . . but I still want to know."

"Never," he said. "I've never brought a girl up here."

"Good."

"Because I just got my own key."

"You rat!" I yelled, grabbing a pillow and swatting him with it.

"Hey . . ." He knocked the pillow out of my hands and pinned me down on the bed. Then he kissed me.

"Let me go, Michael . . . please."

"I can't . . . you're too dangerous."

"I'll be good . . . I promise."

He let go of my arms and I wrapped them around him and we kissed again.

"You're beautiful," he said, looking down at me.

"Don't say things like that . . ."

"Why, do they embarrass you?"

"Yes."

"Okay . . . you're ugly! You're so ugly you make me want to puke." He turned away and leaned over the side of the bed making this terrible retching noise.

"Michael . . . you're crazy . . . stop it . . . I can't stand that!"

"Okay."

We lay next to each other kissing, and soon Michael unbuttoned my sweater and I sat up and unhooked my bra for him. While I slipped out of both, Michael pulled his sweater over his head. Then he held me. "You feel so good," he said, kissing me everywhere. "I love to feel you next to me. You're as soft as Tasha."

I started to laugh.

"What?" Michael asked.

"Nothing . . ."

"I love you, Kath."

"And I love you," I said, "even though you're an *outsy*."

"What's an *outsy*?"

"Your belly button sticks out," I said, tracing it with my fingers.

"That's not the only thing that sticks out."

"Michael . . . we're talking about belly buttons."

"You are . . ."

"I was explaining that you're an *outsy* and I'm an *insy* . . . you see how mine goes in?"

"Umm . . ." he said, kissing it.

"Do belly buttons have a taste?" I asked.

"Yours does . . . it's delicious . . . like the rest of you." He unbuckled my jeans, then his own.

"Michael . . . I'm not sure . . . please . . ."

"Shush . . . don't say anything."

"But Michael . . ."

"Like always, Kath . . . that's all . . ."

We both left on our underpants but after a minute Michael was easing mine down and then his fingers began exploring me. I let my hands wander across his stomach and down his legs and finally I began to stroke Ralph.

"Oh, yes . . . yes . . ." I said, as Michael made me come. And he came too.

We covered up with the patchwork quilt and rested. Michael fell asleep for a while and I watched him, thinking the better you know a person the more you can love him. Do two people ever reach the point where they know absolutely everything there is to know about each other? I leaned over and touched his hair. He didn't move.

The next night Michael picked me up at 7:30 and we headed straight for the apartment. I

knew we would. Neither one of us could wait to
be alone together. And when we were naked,
in each other's arms, I wanted to do everything
—I wanted to feel him inside me. I don't know
if he sensed that or not but when he whispered,
"Please, Kath . . . please let's keep going . . ."
I told him, "Yes, Michael . . . yes . . . but not
here . . . not on the bed."

"Yes . . . here . . ." he said, moving over me.

"No, we can't . . . I might bleed."

He rolled away from me. "You're right . . . I
forgot about that . . . I'll get something."

He came back with a beach towel. "Down
here," I called, because he couldn't find me in
the dark.

"On the floor?" he asked.

"Yes."

"The floor's too hard."

"I don't mind . . . and we won't have to worry
about stains."

"This is crazy."

"Please. Michael . . . just give me the towel
. . . I hope it's not a good one."

He lay down next to me. "It's freezing down
here," he said.

"I know . . ."

He jumped up and grabbed the quilt off the
bed. We snuggled under it. "That's better." He
put his arms around me.

"Look," I said, "you might as well know . . .
I'm scared out of my mind."

"Me too."

"But you've at least had some experience."

"Not with anyone I love."

"Thank you," I said, kissing the side of his face.

He ran his hands up and down my body but nothing happened. I guess I was too nervous. "Michael . . . do you have something?" I asked.

"What for?" he said, nibbling my neck.

"You know . . ."

"Didn't you finish your period?"

"Last week . . . but I'm not taking any chances."

"If you're thinking about VD I promise I'm fine."

"I'm thinking about getting pregnant. Every woman has a different cycle."

"Okay . . . okay . . ." He stood up. "I've got a rubber in my wallet . . . if I can just find it." He looked around for his pants, found them on the floor next to the bed, then had to put on the light to find the rubber. When he did he held it up. "Satisfied?" he asked, turning the light off again.

"I will be when you put it on."

He kneeled beside me and rolled on the rubber. "Anything else?"

"Don't be funny now . . . please . . ."

"I won't . . . I won't . . ." he said and we kissed. Then he was on top of me and I felt Ralph, hard, against my thigh. Just when I thought, Oh God . . . we're really and truly going

to do it, Michael groaned and said, "Oh no . . .
no . . . I'm sorry . . . I'm so sorry . . ."

"What's wrong?"

"I came . . . I don't know what to say. I came
before I even got in. I ruined it . . . I ruined
everything."

"It's all right," I told him. "It's okay . . .
really."

"No, it's not."

"It doesn't matter."

"Maybe not to you . . ."

"It could have been all that talking. We
shouldn't have talked so much."

"Next time it'll be better," Michael said. "I
promise . . . Ralph won't fail me twice."

"Okay." I took his hand and kissed it.

"Let's just sleep for a while, then we can try
again."

"I'm not tired," I said, "but I'm very hungry."

"There's nothing to eat here."

"We could go out."

"Get dressed and go out?"

"Why not?"

"Yeah . . . I suppose we could," he said.

We went to Stanley's for hamburgers and on
the way back to the apartment we stopped at a
drugstore so Michael could buy some more rubbers. I stayed in the car.

"Let's try the living room," Michael said when
we got back.

"I couldn't . . . not on that beautiful rug."

"Oh, hell . . . it's got so many colors nothing would show on it anyway . . . and it's softer than the wood floor."

"I don't know . . ." I said, looking at the rug.

"I'll double up the towel." He spread it out. "There . . . that should take care of it."

This time I tried to relax and think of nothing—nothing but how my body felt—and then Ralph was pushing against me and I whispered, "Are you in . . . are we doing it?"

"Not yet," Michael said, pushing harder. "I don't want to hurt you."

"Don't worry . . . just do it!"

"I'm trying, Kath . . . but it's very tight in there."

"What should I do?"

"Can you spread your legs some more . . . and maybe raise them a little?"

"Like this?"

"That's better . . . much better."

I could feel him halfway inside me and then Michael whispered, "Kath . . ."

"What?"

"I think I'm going to come again."

I felt a big thrust, followed by a quick sharp pain that made me suck in my breath. "Oh . . . oh," Michael cried, but I didn't come. I wasn't even close. "I'm sorry," he said, "I couldn't hold off." He stopped moving. "It wasn't any good for you, was it?"

"Everybody says the first time is no good for

a virgin. I'm not disappointed." But I was. I'd wanted it to be perfect.

"Maybe it was the rubber," Michael said. "I should have bought the more expensive kind." He kissed my cheek and took my hand. "I love you, Kath. I wanted it to be good for you too."

"I know."

"Next time it'll be better . . . we've got to work on it. Did you bleed?"

"I don't feel anything." I wrapped the beach towel around my middle and went to the bathroom. When I wiped myself with tissues I saw a few spots of blood, but nothing like what I'd expected.

On the way home I thought, I am no longer a virgin. I'll never have to go through the first-time business again and I'm glad—I'm so glad it's over! Still, I can't help feeling let down. Everybody makes such a big thing out of actually doing it. But Michael is probably right—this takes practice. I can't imagine what the first time would be like with someone you didn't love.

13

We were sitting around the kitchen table the next day, having Sunday brunch. I thought for sure that as soon as my parents saw me they'd be able to tell. But after a while I realized that they were acting the same as always, so I guess my experience doesn't show, after all.

I smoothed some cream cheese on my bagel and decorated the top with a few dots of lox. My father and Jamie pile their bagels high but I can't eat mine that way. Mom is the same as me. She sort of mashes hers in, making a spread out of it.

When the phone rang, Dad said, "I'll get it . . ." He can reach the wall phone from his seat at the table. "Hello . . . who's calling, please . . . just a minute . . ." He covered the phone with one hand and said, "It's for you, Kath."

"Who is it?"

"Tommy Aronson."

Tommy Aronson? I mouthed his name and my father nodded. "I'll take it upstairs," I said.

I picked up the extension in my parents' bedroom and cleared my throat before I said, "Hello . . ."

"Katherine?"

"Yes?"

"This is Tom Aronson . . . remember me?"

"I remember."

"I'm home for the weekend."

"The weekend's just about over."

"I'm not going back until tomorrow morning."

"Have a nice trip."

"I see you haven't changed."

"Have you?"

"Why don't you come out with me tonight and decide for yourself?"

"Sorry . . . I can't make it."

"Oh, come on . . . I'll behave."

"It's not that . . ."

"Then what?"

"I'm going with someone."

"Oh . . . anyone I know?"

"No."

"Well . . . in that case . . . what's your girlfriend's number?"

"I have a lot of girlfriends."

"The little one . . . you know . . ."

"Erica?"

"That's the one."

"Her last name's Small and she's listed in the book." I hung up before he could say anything else. The nerve of him, coming back into my life today, of all days! And asking for Erica's number just to make me jealous—as if I care one way or the other!

I went back to the kitchen and sat down at the table. My cheeks were burning. "That was Tommy Aronson," I said.

"We know," Mom told me.

"What did he want?" Jamie asked.

"To go out tonight."

"Are you going?"

"Of course not . . . I wouldn't be caught dead with him!"

"You used to like him," Jamie said.

"A long time ago . . . things have changed."

"Is Michael going to be your only boyfriend?"

"For now," Mom answered, before I could. She smiled and offered me another half bagel.

I shook my head. The phone rang again. "That Tommy can't take no for an answer," I said, picking it up. "Hello . . ." I sounded irritated.

"Kath?" It was Michael.

"Oh, hi . . ."

"What's wrong?"

"Nothing . . . I thought you were someone else . . . hang on a second and I'll take it upstairs."

"How're you doing?" he asked me when I picked up the extension.

"I'm fine . . . and you?"

"Okay . . . I just wanted to tell you I thought about you all night."

"Same here . . . about you, that is."

"And that it was very special for me."

"For me, too . . ."

My mother came to my room that night. "I cut this article out of today's *Times*," she said, handing it to me. "I think it has a lot to say . . . you might find it interesting."

I got comfortable in bed, adjusted my lamp, and looked at the article. Maybe Mom could tell about me after all. The title was *What about the right to say 'no'?* and the subtitle was *Sexual liberation*. It was written by the director of medical clinics at Yale. He said that he always asks adolescents (am I still considered an adolescent?) four questions when he talks to them about sex.

1—Is sexual intercourse necessary for the relationship?

2—What should you expect from sexual intercourse?

3—If you should need help, where will you seek it?

4—Have you thought about how this relationship will end?

He went on to explain each question. In his discussion of question two he said that *enjoyable love-making, culminating in orgasm, isn't easy. It usually requires mutual education. It takes time, effort, and patience to learn to make love.*

That made me feel better about last night.

It's funny, because I used to think if you read enough books you'd automatically know how to do everything the right way. But reading and doing are not the same at all.

Question three didn't interest me that much so I jumped ahead to question four, which made me very angry. Why should I have to think about *the end* with Michael when we are just at *the beginning?* And I didn't like the way he said, *Rejection is rejection whether we call it divorce, puppy love or adolescent turmoil.* Anyway, who says a relationship has to end?

"What did you think?" Mom asked over breakfast.

"About what?"

"That article?"

"Oh . . . well, it was pretty good."

"Did you agree?"

"With some of it . . . like a person shouldn't ever feel pushed into sex . . . or that she has to do it to please someone else . . ."

"I'm glad you feel that way," Mom said.

"I'm answering you hypothetically," I told her, "not personally."

"Yes, of course."

"You'll never believe who called me yesterday," Erica said. We were sitting in English, which we both have second period. Mr. Frazier wasn't there yet.

"Tommy Aronson?" I asked.

"He called you first?"

I could see that Erica was surprised, and hurt too. "Just to get your number," I said.

"Oh, wow . . . for a minute I really wondered."

"Did you go out with him?"

"No . . . but he came over." Erica must have seen some expression on my face that made her add, "We didn't make out, if that's what you're thinking."

"I'm not thinking anything . . . what you do is your own business."

"Not that he didn't try," Erica said, "and not that I wasn't curious . . . he has a very sexy body."

"So how come you didn't?"

"Because he's so dull . . . he doesn't have an idea in his head. Compared to Artie he's a real nothing . . . even if he does have a perpetual hard-on."

We both laughed as Mr. Frazier walked into the room, smoothing down his hair. His zipper was at half-mast, as usual.

I was surprised that Erica didn't say anything about the fact that I am no longer a virgin. She said she'd be able to tell in a minute. I was sure she'd ask me all about it. So in a way I will always be grateful to Tommy Aronson because if she hadn't had him on her mind she'd have put me through the third degree. And I'm not sure that I'd have told her the truth.

About school, I have two things to say. One,

senior year is a bore, except for activities and history, and two, everyone is just marking time until graduation and all the teachers know it.

About my other friends, which I also haven't mentioned, I already know that after graduation we won't be seeing much of each other. It's funny how you can grow away from your friends, when just a few years ago they were the most important people in your life. We used to travel in a pack—there were eight of us and we did everything together. We still share a table at lunch but I don't talk to them on the phone every night, the way I used to, and I certainly don't share my innermost thoughts with them either. Erica is the only one of them I really care about now.

I used to be best friends with Janis Foster. Since ninth grade Janis has been going with Mark Fiore. He's finishing his first year at Rutgers now. Naturally Janis is going to Douglass. She and Mark have their entire lives mapped out. They know exactly when they're going to get married and exactly when Baby One and Baby Two will be born. They've even picked out names. Sometimes, on Sundays, they go looking at houses, and at lunch on Monday Janis will tell us they know just where they want to live seven years from now. They make life seem so dull.

Lately, avoiding Janis and Mark has been tricky. She knows I'm going with Michael and wants to meet him. We're in modern dance together and Janis is always after me to make plans for us to go out together. I'm running out of excuses. Maybe it's selfish, but I don't want to waste a night with Michael by spending it with them. She must be really dense not to get the picture.

That night Michael called right after dinner. "Can I come over . . . just for a little while?"

"I have to finish a paper on Somerset Maugham," I told him.

"I'll only stay an hour. I miss you, Kath."

"I miss you too," I whispered.

"See you in a little while."

"Okay."

I raced upstairs and took a shower and shampoo. If I don't wash my hair at least every other day it gets oily and looks terrible. I put on a fresh pair of jeans and a sweatshirt.

"I brought my books," Michael said, after we'd kissed hello.

"Good . . . because if I don't get this paper in by Friday I'm going to fail. We can work at the kitchen table."

As soon as we got our books arranged Jamie wandered in. "I want a pretzel," she said.

"Take the box and please leave," I told her.

"Okay . . . okay . . ."

A few minutes later she was back. "They made me thirsty . . . I need some juice."

"Jamie . . ."

"Okay . . . I can take a hint."

"It's not that we don't want you in here," Michael told her. "It's just that we have a lot of studying to do."

"Sure."

At 10:00 Michael gathered his books and I walked him out to his car. "Get in for a minute," he said.

We put our arms around each other and kissed. "I don't know how I'll last until Friday," Michael said. "I can't think of anything else."

"Me neither."

We kissed again.

Like my mother said, you can't go back to holding hands and anyway, I don't want to.

14

⋘◉⦙◉⋙

"There's no school on Friday," Erica said. We were in the locker room, changing into our gym-suits.

"I know . . . some kind of special teacher's meeting."

"So you want to see a preview of a new Robert Redford picture?"

"Are you kidding? I'd love to!"

"We're taking the 8:45 train."

"I'll meet you at the station."

"No . . . we can pick you up . . . say around 8:30."

"Great . . . and tell your mother thanks for asking me."

When I got home from school I found a small package in the mail, from my grandmother. As I ripped it open I wondered if it could be a birthday present two weeks early. As soon as I saw what was inside I knew it wasn't. First I read the note.

Dear Kath,

I hear that you and Michael are officially go-
ing together. Thought these might come in
handy. And remember, if you ever need to talk,
I'm available. I don't judge, I just advise.

                    Love,
                    Grandma

I pulled out a whole bunch of pamphlets from
Planned Parenthood on birth control, abortion
and venereal disease.

At first I was angry. Grandma is jumping to
conclusions again, I thought. But then I sat
down and started to read. It turned out she had
sent me a lot of valuable information. Could
my mother have put her up to it?

I went to the phone and dialed her office.

"Gross, Gross and Gross . . . Good afternoon . . ."

"Haillie Gross, please," I said.

"Who's calling?"

"Katherine Danziger."

"One moment . . ."

"Kath?" It was Grandma.

"Hi," I said. "I got the stuff you sent."

"That was fast. I just mailed it yesterday."

"It was here when I got home from school."

"You're not angry, are you?" Grandma asked.

"Me? Why should I be angry?"

"You shouldn't be . . . but sometimes you
jump to conclusions."

"Me . . . jump to conclusions?"

"You."

"Look . . . I'm glad you sent that stuff . . . it's very interesting . . . not personally or anything . . . but in general."

"I'm glad you think so. Do me a favor though . . . don't tell your mother and father . . ."

"Why not?"

"Sometimes it's hard for parents to accept the facts . . . so let's keep it between the two of us, okay?"

"Sure . . . okay. I'm coming into New York on Friday . . . maybe I could meet you and Grandpa for lunch."

"We'd love it," she said. "I'll make a reservation at Basil's . . . 12:30?"

"Fine."

"See you then."

"Right . . . bye."

That night I got into bed early and read all the pamphlets. When I'd finished I thought, well, I can start a service in school I know so much, which might not be a bad idea, considering there is a girl in my gym class who, until this year, never knew that intercourse was how you got pregnant, and she's already done it!

The next morning, during study hall, I went to the phone booth near the office and called Planned Parenthood of New York City. The phone rang three times before anyone answered.

Either it was very hot in the booth or I was nervous because all of a sudden I was sweating like crazy.

"Hello . . . can I help you?"

"Yes," I said, coughing twice. "I'd like some information about birth control . . . that is, about getting it."

"One moment please . . ."

She connected me with someone else. "You wish to make an appointment?"

"I guess so."

"May I ask your age?"

"Does it matter?"

"No . . . we don't require parental permission . . . but if you're a teenager we have special sessions."

"Oh . . . I'll be eighteen in two weeks."

"Then you could come in this Thursday at 4:00."

"I was hoping I could get an appointment for Friday. You see, I live in New Jersey and I'll be in the city then."

"Hold on a minute, please." I heard a click. After a few seconds she came back on the line. "Friday afternoon will be fine."

"Oh, that's great."

"Your name, please?"

"Katherine Danziger."

"Would you spell the last name?"

"D-a-n-z-i-g-e-r."

"Very good . . . come to the Margaret Sanger Clinic at 22nd Street and 2nd Avenue at 3:00."

"Thank you . . . I'll be there."

On Friday morning my father asked me if I needed any money for my day in New York.

"I've got some saved up," I told him.

"Then use this for train fare," he said, handing me a five.

"Thanks, Dad."

"And have a nice day."

Going to a private screening with Juliette Small is a lot different than just going to the movies. This was the third time she'd invited me to join her. I like Mrs. Small. She acts like a regular person. You would never know she's famous. There were about twenty-five other people at the screening, besides us, and Erica said most of them were reviewers, like her mother.

After the picture Mrs. Small asked me, personally, what I thought of it.

"Well . . ." I told her, "I just love Robert Redford."

"Don't we all . . ." Mrs. Small said, "but I mean about the story."

"Oh, the story . . . I liked it . . ."

"But . . ."

"I don't think it could happen that way in real life . . ."

"Exactly!" she said. "But you wanted it to, didn't you . . . you were hoping it would turn out just that way."

"Yes," I told her.

"You see . . . that's the whole point."

"It's going to be a smash," Erica said.

"In spite of my review, you mean?"

"In spite of anybody's review."

"I agree with you, completely," Mrs. Small said. She got into her coat. "Well, that wraps it up . . . I'm yours for the rest of the day. Where shall we begin . . . the Guggenheim, the Whitney . . ."

"How about lunch?" Erica said.

"You're hungry already?"

"Famished . . ."

"Then lunch it is. Kath, want to join us?"

"Oh, thanks . . . but I'm meeting my grandparents."

"Of course . . . Erica did tell me that . . . how are they?"

"Just fine."

"Good . . . send them my love, will you?"

"I will. And thanks a lot for the show. I really enjoyed it."

Outside, I grabbed a cab and gave the driver the address of Basil's. It's my grandparents' favorite restaurant—a very small East Side place where Basil, the owner, will fix special dishes for his regular customers, like Grandpa, who's on a low sodium diet.

They were waiting for me in a booth, in the back, where they like to sit. Grandpa looked pale. I kissed him on the cheek, then hugged Grandma. She was wearing a big yellow felt hat. "Hey . . . I like that," I told her.

"It hides my hair," she said. "Whenever I need a shampoo I wear it."

Basil took our order himself and when I asked him about the special of the day, Chicken Kiev, he whipped out his pencil and drew a picture of it for me, right on the tablecloth, all the time explaining exactly how it's prepared. After that I felt I had to order it.

"So . . ." Grandma said, when Basil had finished with us, "let me get a good look at you." She narrowed her eyes and inspected me. I tried to keep a straight face. Finally she said, "Wonderful . . . glowing . . ."

"Oh, Grandma . . . people don't really glow . . . that's such a silly expression."

"What do you mean people don't really glow? Of course they do. Don't be embarrassed . . . it's very becoming." She looked across the table at Grandpa. "Doesn't she glow, Ivan?"

"To me, Katherine always glows," Grandpa said slowly.

"It must be love," Grandma said.

I could tell I was blushing, even though I didn't want to.

Grandpa raised his water glass. "To love . . ." he said.

Grandma clinked her glass against his. "To love . . ."

After dessert, Grandma and I went to the Ladies' Room. I thought about telling her that I have a 3:00 appointment at the Margaret Sanger Clinic. I knew she'd be pleased. But I decided against it because I want it to be my own experience, one I don't have to share with anyone, except Michael.

We said goodbye to Basil and went outside. It had turned very warm, like a beautiful spring day.

"Whew . . ." Grandma said, unbuttoning her coat. "I'm going back to the office for an hour. I have some work to finish . . ."

I checked my watch. "Well . . . I guess I'll be taking off now. I have a lot of shopping to do." I kissed them both goodbye. "Thanks for lunch." Grandpa hugged me extra hard.

I watched as Grandma helped him into a cab, then I started walking. There's something about walking in New York that really appeals to me, especially on a bright sunny day. I took off my jacket and hung it over my arm. I felt like smiling at everyone on the street even though I know you shouldn't do that in New York. It could lead to big trouble.

15

I got to the clinic at 2:45. I went inside and gave my name to the receptionist. There were seven other people in my group session, including two young couples. First we had a general discussion with a physician and a social worker. They explained all the methods of birth control. You could ask questions if you wanted. I didn't.

Next came a private session called Personal Counseling—just me and a social worker. She was young and very pretty with long hair, tied back, and tinted glasses. Her name was Linda Kolker. I wondered if she was sexually experienced and decided she must be or else she wouldn't have the job.

We talked about the weather and my family for a minute and then she asked me my reason for coming to the clinic.

I told her, "I think it's my responsibility to make sure I don't get pregnant."

She nodded and said, "Do you have one special boyfriend?"

"Yes."

"Have you discussed this with him?"

"Not really."

"How do you think he'll feel about it?"

"I'm sure he'll be very happy. He approves of birth control."

"But coming here was all your idea?"

"Yes . . . absolutely."

"Good. Some of the questions I have to ask you are rather personal, Katherine . . . so that we can determine what method of birth control will be best for you."

"I understand."

"Have you already had sexual intercourse?"

"Yes."

"Have you been using a birth control device?"

"Yes."

"Which one?"

"A rubber . . . that is, a condom."

"Combined with foam or by itself?"

"By itself."

"And you find that method unacceptable?"

"Well . . . it's hard for me to say because we just did it one time."

"Oh . . . I see . . ."

Now I nodded.

"But you plan to have intercourse regularly?"

"Yes."

"About how often?"

"How often?" I repeated.

"Yes . . . how often do you plan to have intercourse?"

"Well . . . I don't know exactly."

"Would you say weekends and holidays or every day or once a month or a few times a year?"

"I guess on weekends mainly."

"Do you think you'll know in advance or will it be a spontaneous decision?"

"I guess I'll know in advance."

"Okay . . . so much for that. I'll need a little medical history now. How old were you when you began to menstruate?"

"Almost fourteen."

"And are your periods regular?"

"Sort of . . . I get it every four to five weeks."

"And how long does each period last?"

"About five days."

"Any bleeding in between periods?"

"No."

"Vaginal discharge?"

"Sometimes."

"Color?"

"Just clear."

"That's normal . . . any severe cramping?"

"No . . . just some low back pain the first day . . . nothing bad."

"How about your mother . . . is she in good health?"

"Yes, she's fine."

"Does she take birth control pills?"

"No . . . she uses a diaphragm."

"Quite a good method if it's used properly."

"I'd rather take the Pill."

"Yes . . . it has esthetic advantages but it's not the answer for everyone." I guess I must have looked unhappy when she said that because she added, "We'll see what the doctor has to say . . . okay? The whole idea of coming here is to find the birth control device that best suits the individual."

I nodded again.

"Now then . . . I need your written consent for the gonorrhea culture . . ." She hesitated for a moment, then added, "It's simple and painless."

"But I can't possibly have gonorrhea," I told her.

"There's always a possibility . . . and it's often difficult for the woman to tell . . ."

"But Michael . . . besides . . ."

"Look . . . it only takes a few seconds and it's so much safer to be sure . . ."

"All right," I said, deciding it was easier to agree. I signed my name. I tried not to think of Michael and that girl on the beach in Maine.

"Good," she said, standing up. She held out her hand and I shook it. "I'll see you after your physical, Katherine."

"Okay," I said. "And thank you."

My physical consisted of weight and blood pressure, a routine breast exam, with the doctor explaining how I should check my breasts each month, then my first pelvic examination. I tried to act as if I was used to it, but I didn't fool the doctor, who said, "Try to relax, Kather-

ine. This isn't going to hurt." And it didn't
either, but it was uncomfortable for a minute,
like when he pushed with one hand from inside and with the other from outside.

Then he slipped this cold thing into my vagina and explained, "This is a vaginal speculum.
It holds the walls of the vagina open so that the
inside is easily seen. Would you like to see your
cervix?"

"I don't know . . ."

"I think it's a good idea to become familiar
with your body."

He held a mirror between my legs and I
looked down while he explained what I was
seeing. It reminded me of the time that Erica
taught me to use tampons. I had to hold a mirror between my legs then too, to find the right
hole.

"That's interesting," I told the doctor.

"Yes . . . the human body never ceases to
amaze me." He took the mirror away and I lay
back on the table.

"I'm almost done now, Katherine . . . just a
Pap smear . . . there," he said, passing a long
Q-tip kind of thing to his assistant. "And the
gonorrhea culture . . . okay . . . that does it."
He took off his rubber glove. "Now . . . do you
have any preference concerning birth control
devices?"

"Yes," I told him. "I'd like to try the Pill."

"I don't see any reason why you shouldn't . . .
you're in excellent health . . . get dressed now

and Ms. Kolker will see you back in her office."

"How did it go?" she asked.

"Oh, it was nothing," I told her.

"Here's your prescription." She passed it across her desk, then gave me a two-month supply of pills with instructions, making sure I understood every detail. We also discussed possible side-effects, in which case I am to call the clinic immediately.

I took a taxi to Penn Station and caught the 5:17 train. I couldn't wait to tell Michael my news.

But when I got home my mother said, "Michael called . . . he's got the flu."

16

Two days later I came down with the same bug. My temperature went up to 104°. I could barely swallow, my head hurt something awful and I was so weak and dizzy I couldn't make it to the bathroom by myself. The doctor prescribed aspirin, bed rest and plenty to drink.

I felt like I was dying.

Mom and Dad took turns staying home from work to take care of me. My father is a super nurse. He concocts delicious fruit drinks in the blender, knows just when you need a cold compress on your head, and loves to play gin rummy.

I stayed in bed for four days. Jamie wasn't allowed anywhere near me but every night she stood in my doorway and told me about her day. On Thursday I got up for an hour and walked around. I'd lost five pounds and had no strength. That night I called Michael.

"Hi . . . how are you?" he asked.

"I'm a lot better . . . I walked around for a

while today and tomorrow I'm getting out of bed
for good."

"Don't be surprised if you feel like jumping
back in . . ." He coughed.

"You don't sound so good . . . can't you take
something for that?"

"Yeah . . . I've got a whole mess of stuff."

"I miss you," I said.

"You wouldn't if you could see me . . . I look
like the creature from the green lagoon."

"I don't look so good myself. Are you going
back to school tomorrow?"

"No . . . not till Monday."

"Can you come over this weekend?"

"I hope so . . . I'll call you tomorrow and let
you know."

"Okay . . . and take it easy."

"You too." He coughed again.

On Sunday afternoon he was well enough to
drive over for a short visit. I begged Mom to
let me wash my hair but she wouldn't. So I
tucked it up inside a beach hat, remembering
that's what Grandma does. I knew I looked awful but so did he. He had dark circles under his
eyes.

"What's with the hat?" he asked.

"It's hiding my hair . . . I don't want you to
see it this way."

"You think it'd make a difference?"

"It might."

"You look tired."

"And you look green," I said, starting to laugh.

"I told you, didn't I?" He laughed with me until he started to cough. "Want a coughdrop?" he asked, popping one into his mouth.

"Thanks."

We sat in the den, holding hands, listening to music and talking.

I waited until my birthday, the following Friday, to tell Michael about the Pill. He had planned a special celebration. First we went to see *Candide* at the Paper Mill Playhouse and then we stopped at Mario's for a spaghetti supper. When we were just about through Michael reached into his pocket and pulled out a small black jewelry box. "Happy birthday," he said, pushing it across the table.

"For me?" I never know how to act when I get a present. I'm always embarrassed. "What is it?"

"Open the box."

"Okay . . ." I opened it slowly. Inside was a small silver disk, with *Katherine* engraved across it, on a slender silver chain. "Oh, Michael . . . it's just beautiful."

"Turn it over," he told me.

I did, and on the other side it said, *Forever ... Michael.* Right away I knew I was going to cry. I bit my lip and tried to hold back the tears but nothing worked.

Michael called for the check while I hid my face behind a napkin. "I guess I should have waited till we were alone," he said.

I couldn't answer.

"Hey, Kath . . . come on . . . cut it out, will you . . ."

I nodded to show I was trying.

"It was supposed to make you happy . . . not sad."

"I'm not sad," I said in a squeaky voice.

"Let's get out of here." Michael paid the check, steered me through the restaurant, and led me to the car.

When we were inside he fastened the chain around my neck and kissed me. I looked down at the silver disk, touched it and said, "In my whole life nothing will ever mean more to me."

"I'm glad you like it."

We kissed again and then I whispered in his ear, "I've got a surprise for you, too."

"My birthday's still a month away."

"I know . . . this is a different kind of surprise."

"Oh, yeah . . . tell me . . ."

"You have to guess."

"At least give me a hint."

"Okay . . . it's something I've got."

"VD?" he asked.

I swatted him over the head with my pocket-book. "Not unless you gave it to me!"

"No chance."

"Then guess again."

"I'm no good at guessing games."

"Oh . . . all right," I said, opening my pocket-book. I took out a package of pills and held them up for him to see.

At first he didn't seem to understand but then this slow smile spread across his face and he said, "The Pill?"

"Yup."

"You're taking the Pill?"

"Uh huh."

"Since when?"

"I got them the day you got sick."

"But where . . . how . . ."

"I went to Planned Parenthood in New York."

"You're full of surprises, aren't you?"

"Well, it makes sense, doesn't it?"

"Oh, yeah . . . a lot."

I'd promised my parents we'd come home early, since according to them, I was still recuperating from the flu. They'd had friends in for dinner and everyone was still there when we got back, so Michael and I had no chance to be alone. We kissed goodnight on the front porch.

"Are Sharon and Ike away for the weekend?" I asked.

"No . . ."

"Oh . . . that's too bad." I put my arms around his waist and looked up at him.

"Don't worry," Michael said, "I'll think of something."

"Not your house," I told him the next night when he called for me, "I couldn't . . ."

"Why not? My mother and father won't be home before 12:00."

I checked my watch. It was 7:30. "I don't know . . ." I said. "I feel funny about going to your house."

"Look," he said, "we don't have to do anything . . . we can just go there and talk."

"I think I've heard that before!"

Michael's house is red brick with white shutters. It's near the company where his father works. As soon as he unlocked the front door Tasha jumped on me. "Hi, Tasha . . ." I patted her head.

"Down girl," Michael said, and Tasha obeyed. "Come on . . ." He took my hand and showed me around. Everything was very neat. Their furniture was big, heavy and dark and the drapes were drawn in the living and dining rooms.

The kitchen was brighter, with yellow wallpaper, and hanging plants. A note was attached to the refrigerator with a magnetic flower. It said, *M—soup in refrig. Heat, don't boil.*

"Want to see my room?" Michael asked.

"As long as I'm here I might as well," I laughed.

He led me upstairs, down a long hallway, to a room with cluttered bookcases and an unmade bed.

"Sorry about that," he said. "I'm supposed to make it every day but sometimes I forget."

"How can anybody forget to make a bed?"

"It's easy." He turned on some music while

I walked around inspecting all the things on his shelves. He had lots of paperbacks, some team pennants, a picture of a chimpanzee dressed in jeans—his family must be very big on monkeys, I thought—and a cartoon showing a little boy, spelling out f-u-c-k with his alphabet soup. I held up a camp trophy. "Congratulations," I said, ". . . Most Improved Swimmer . . . wow!"

"Yeah . . . that was the year I got brave enough to jump into the deep water." We both laughed while Tasha curled up in the corner, under a chair.

"Can I look in your closet?" I asked.

"Sure . . . help yourself," Michael said and he began to straighten his bed.

I opened the closet. The floor was piled high with shoes, sports equipment and, I think, dirty laundry.

"Find what you're looking for?" he said.

"I'm not looking for anything special. I want to see everything . . . I want to know you inside out. So far I've discovered you're a slob."

"Only about some things," he said.

I opened what I thought was a second closet but it turned out to be a bathroom. There were towels strewn all around which Michael picked up in a hurry and dumped into the hamper.

"God . . ." I said, going through his bathroom cabinet, "you use more junk than I do." There were three kinds of deodorant, two shampoos, a tube of athlete's foot cream, acne soaps, medicated skin lotions, several prescriptions, and at least six different kinds of after shaves. "No wonder you always smell different," I said.

"Pick out your favorite and I'll throw the rest away."

"I don't know one from the other," I said, lining them up on the counter. I took off all the tops and started sniffing. "I like this one." I held up a bottle of green lotion called *Moustache*.

"You would . . . that's the most expensive of the lot."

"Mmmm . . ." I said, sniffing it again. "I have good taste."

He took the bottle from me and splashed some on his face.

"Do you ever put it on your balls?" I asked.

"I don't shave them," he said.

"I read that in a book . . . this guy put after shave on his balls before he went out with his girlfriends."

"Well . . . maybe I would too . . . if I thought anybody was going to smell them."

"Who did you have in mind?"

"Oh, I don't know . . . just anybody." He put the bottle on top of the toilet and unbuckled his jeans.

"What are you doing?"

"I'm going to try it now . . . so I'm ready . . . just in case." He stepped out of his jeans, then took off his underpants. "On second thought," he said, "why don't you do it for me?"

"Me . . . ?"

"It was your idea in the first place."

I felt funny about seeing Michael exposed from the waist down, because it's always been dark when we make love. I've touched him a lot but I've never looked carefully.

He sensed my feelings because he said, "You want to know me inside out, don't you?"

So I looked. His hair down there is almost the same color as on his head, but curlier. Mine is very dark, much darker than on my head. "Hello, Ralph . . ." I said, kneeling in front of Michael. Ralph was small and soft and just hung there. I shook some *Moustache* into the palm of my hand but when I reached out toward Michael, he caught my hand and said, "Don't . . . it stings . . ."

"How do you know?"

"I just do . . ."

"But you said . . ." He didn't let me finish. Instead, he kneeled with me and as we kissed Ralph grew bigger and hard. I undressed myself, while Michael watched. Ralph stuck straight out, as if he was watching too. We made love on the bathroom rug, but just when I was getting really excited, Michael came. I wondered if it would ever work out right between us.

"I'm sorry," he said. "I just couldn't wait . . . it's been a few weeks."

"That's okay."

We got into his bed and fell asleep for an hour and when we woke up Ralph was hard again. This time Michael made it last much, much longer and I got so carried away I grabbed

his backside with both hands, trying to push
him deeper and deeper into me—and I spread
my legs as far apart as I could—and I raised
my hips off the bed—and I moved with him,
again and again and again—and at last, I came.
I came right before Michael and as I did I made
noises, just like my mother. Michael did too.

While he was still on top of me, catching his
breath, I started laughing. "I came . . ." I told
him. "I actually came."

"I know," he said, "I felt it . . . is that what's
so funny?"

"I don't know why I'm laughing."

"Did you like it, Kath?"

"What a question . . . I felt so close to you . . .
I've never felt so close to you before."

"Same here."

"Can we do it again?" I asked.

"Not right now . . . I've got to rest for a
while."

"Oh. Michael . . ."

"Yeah?"

"How'd Ralph get his name?"

He looked at me and smiled. "I named him
just for you."

Tasha jumped up on the bed and snuggled
next to Michael. I'd forgotten she was in the
room. Michael petted her for a few minutes,
then put his arm around me and fell asleep
again. I watched him. I love to watch him while
he sleeps. Besides everything else he is really my
best friend now. It's a different kind of friend-

ship from the one I have with Erica. It makes me wish I could share every day with him—forever.

After half an hour I shook him gently. "It's 10:30," I said.

"Mmm . . . we better get going."

"I'm starving," I told him.

"Me too."

"I need a shower."

"Want company?"

"That'll be fun . . . are you sure we have enough time?"

"If we hurry."

We went into the bathroom and Michael got clean towels out for both of us and adjusted the water over the tub. "Do you always wear your necklace in the shower?" he asked.

"Of course," I said. "I never take it off."

He soaped my back. Then I did his.

We dried each other off and I used one of his deodorants. He put *Moustache* on his face, then we got dressed and went out for something to eat.

Over hamburgers I asked him, "Well . . . how does it feel to have made it with an older woman?" He gave me a blank look so I added, "I'm eighteen now, remember? But you won't be for another month."

He polished off his Coke. "There's a lot to be said for older women!"

On the way back to my house I said, "I'd like to meet your parents."

"You will . . . one of these days."

"What are they like?"

"They're okay . . . a little stuffier than yours, but basically they're good guys."

"What would they say if they knew about us?"

"My mother would think you'd seduced me . . . and my father would say I've got good taste."

"Oh, you!"

When we got to my house we sat in the den for an hour—otherwise my parents might have been suspicious. I thought how nice it would be if we could just go upstairs, to bed, together. I was hoping we'd make love again but Michael said he was kind of exhausted. Probably from just getting over the flu.

17

Jamie is in love. His name is David and he's in her math class. She says he looks a lot like Michael. They've decided to act as if they hate each other in public so no one will be able to guess the truth and tease them. When I hear that I'm glad I'm not thirteen anymore. He's been calling Jamie every night, tying up the phone for ages, which makes it hard for Michael to get through to me. So my parents have limited both our calls to fifteen minutes each.

This summer Jamie is going back to camp in New Hampshire. She says she can't wait. It doesn't seem to matter to her that she won't see David for seven weeks, which proves that love at thirteen is nothing like love at eighteen.

I don't know what I'm going to do about the summer. I've been job hunting, but so far, no luck. Mrs. Handelsman says I shouldn't worry, that something will turn up by June. But it's already the middle of April and I'm worried. So is Michael. He hasn't found anything either and he's counting on a good summer salary to help with next year's expenses at school.

On Monday morning Erica was waiting outside my homeroom. "I got the job on *The Leader*," she said.

The Leader is Westfield's weekly newspaper. There were at least a hundred kids after that job. "You're really lucky," I told her. "I wish I could find something exciting like that."

On Tuesday morning she was waiting for me again. "Sybil's pregnant," she said, shifting her books from one arm to the other. "I found out last night."

"Oh no . . ."

"And she doesn't know who the father is."

"Oh God . . ."

"And she's too far gone to have an abortion . . . the baby's due in early July."

I counted on my fingers. "That means she got pregnant in October . . ."

"Uh huh . . . and never even missed a day of school."

"Jesus . . . why didn't she say anything?"

"She wanted to have the baby and she knew if her parents found out they'd make her have an abortion."

"You mean they didn't notice?"

"She's so fat . . . you know . . . she just kept wearing those tents of hers and nothing showed . . ."

"Didn't she go to a doctor?"

"Yeah . . . but she told him she was married and gave him a phony name and address . . ."

"What's she going to do with a baby?"

"Oh, she knows she can't keep it. She'll put it up for adoption as soon as it's born."

"Then why have it in the first place?"

"For the experience, she told me."

"Will she be able to graduate?"

"I guess so . . . nobody knows but my aunt and uncle, my parents and us. And the only reason she told in the first place was they wanted to send her to Duke University for the summer . . . to this fat people's clinic."

I shook my head. "I can't believe it."

"I know . . . neither can I."

"I'd have an abortion . . . wouldn't you?"

"In a minute . . . my mother's so worked up about Sybil she made an appointment for me to see her gynecologist . . . she wants me to take the Pill. I told her, *Relax, Mom—I'm still a virgin,* but she said she'd feel better if she knew that I was prepared for college, in every way."

"Are you going to take it?"

"Sure . . . I like the idea of being ready for anything . . . and maybe it'll even help Artie . . . make him feel more secure."

The last Thursday in April is Career Day at our school. This year I was hostess to Sharon and my grandmother so I got to eat lunch in the teachers' cafeteria. The food wasn't any better there. Grandma and Sharon hit it off very well, trading anecdotes about their work.

After lunch there was a special assembly and all the guests gave short talks about their careers. Then the audience split up into groups and visited with the three speakers of their choice. Both Grandma and Sharon were among the most popular and had full classrooms at all three sessions.

At the end of the day Mrs. Handelsman couldn't thank me enough. We walked back to her office together. "I've been waiting to hear from you about those extra schools," she said. "What ever happened?"

"My parents wouldn't give me permission," I answered.

She touched my shoulder. "I'm sure everything will work out for the best."

"I hope so."

I didn't tell her that Michael and I have another plan. Since both the University of Vermont and Middlebury are on the trimester system, he will take off the winter semester and teach skiing in Colorado. He'll make up the lost credits at summer school and that way he can still graduate in four years and we can be together every weekend, all winter long. He's already written to Vail, Aspen and Steamboat Springs, stating his qualifications.

"But suppose I'm not accepted at Denver?" I said to him.

"You'll be accepted . . . don't worry."

So on Career Day my mind wasn't really on Sharon or Grandma or any other speakers.

There was just one thing I could think about—
college acceptances—which were due in the
mail any day.

Two days later they arrived and I was rejected
at Michigan, but accepted at Penn State and
Denver. Michael got into University of Vermont
but not Middlebury. A week after we heard
from our schools, Erica was accepted at Radcliffe.

"I'm really not surprised," she said, when I
called to congratulate her. "Did you hear about
Sybil?"

"No . . . what now?"

"She got into Smith, Wellesley, Holyoke and
Stanford . . . everywhere she applied. She didn't
tell them she was pregnant."

"She's too much . . . What about Artie?" I
asked, "anything new?"

"So far he's on the waiting list at Temple but
that's it."

"Maybe if he's not accepted anywhere else
his father will change his mind and let him go
to the American Academy."

"That's what I said but Artie doesn't believe
it."

I wrote to Denver right way, accepting, even
though my parents felt I should wait a few
weeks and think it over since Denver is so far
away. Then I explained to them about Michael's
plan. They weren't overjoyed.

18

When the weather turns warm we have a salad for supper once a week—tunafish, hard-boiled eggs, cheese and raw vegetables—usually on Wednesdays, because that's my mother's late day at the library.

I was peeling foil off a wedge of cheese when my father said, "How would you like to play tennis all summer *and* get paid for it?"

"Are you kidding . . . I'd love it," I told him, popping the cheese into my mouth.

He smiled. "I was hoping you'd say that."

"You're serious?" I asked. "Is the tennis club looking for someone?"

"No . . . but Foxy is."

"Foxy?"

"Sam Fox . . . the director of Jamie's camp," Dad said. "I spoke to him this morning . . . he's built three new courts . . . all weather composition . . . and he needs an assistant tennis counselor . . . the boy he originally hired has hepatitis."

"I can't go to Jamie's camp," I said, spearing an egg yolk.

"He'll pay you $350," Dad said.

"I don't care if it's $3000 . . . I'm not going to New Hampshire."

Mom and Dad exchanged looks.

"It's out of the question," I told them, suddenly having trouble getting the egg down.

"I told Foxy I was sure you'd be interested in the job . . ."

"Well, you can tell him you were wrong!"

"May I be excused?" Jamie asked.

"Go ahead," my mother said. When she was gone Mom turned to me. "Daddy went to a lot of trouble to find you a good job."

"Who asked him to?"

My mother put down her knife and fork. "I can't say I like your attitude."

I fought back tears. "Do you think I'm stupid . . . do you think I can't see what you're trying to do . . ."

"This had nothing to do with Michael," my father said.

"Don't lie . . . please!"

"All right," Mom said. "We both think you could use a change of scenery . . ."

"A change of scenery! Did you forget I'm going to Denver . . . you know Michael and I only have until September."

"Camp is just seven weeks," my father said.

"Just seven weeks!"

"Will you stop repeating everything I say," Dad shouted.

"Seven weeks may not be a lot to you but to me it's forever!"

"Let's try to discuss this rationally," Mom said.

My father lowered his voice. "Look, Kath . . . I already told Foxy it was a deal . . . that you'd take the job."

"You told him! What right have you to answer for me? I'm not a child anymore . . . I'm eighteen . . . " I didn't care that I was crying now. I wiped my nose and eyes with my dinner napkin.

"Last summer you said you'd love to be a counselor at Jamie's camp," Mom reminded me.

"That was last summer . . . things have changed!"

"I'd like you to give it some thought," Dad said.

"I already have . . . and my mind's made up . . . so you can call Foxy and tell him to find somebody else." I threw down my napkin and stood up.

"No," my father said. It hit me then that his mind was made up too. I understood the whole thing, just like that. "Let me get this straight," I said, very slowly. "You're telling me that I have no choice . . . is that right?"

"That's right," Dad said.

"Mom . . ." I began.

"I think you should give it a try," she said.

"What does that mean . . . an hour, a day, a week . . ."

"I think you should go for the summer."

"I can't believe this," I said. "I always thought you were really fair . . . both of you . . . but I can see I was wrong . . . way wrong . . ."

"I know how it seems now, Kath . . ." Mom said.

I held up a hand. "Don't feed me any of that crap about how grateful I'll be when I'm older . . ."

"I wasn't going to . . ." she answered, but I didn't stick around to listen. I ran out of the kitchen and upstairs, to my bedroom.

I was all cried out when Jamie knocked on my door, later. "I don't think they should make you go," she said.

"Did you tell them that?"

"Yes."

"And?"

"They said I should stay out of it."

"I could just walk out of here . . . I wonder if they ever thought of that . . . I could just pack my things and take off . . ."

"You won't though . . . will you?" Jamie asked. She looked really worried.

I rolled over on my bed and sighed. "No . . . I guess not . . ." It's strange, but when it comes right down to it I never do fall part—even when I'm sure I will.

"I'm glad," Jamie said.

We didn't discuss the situation at home the

next day or the day after that but it was understood that I would take the job at camp.

And now I had to tell Michael.

I thought about waiting until his birthday. It's just a week away. I opened my bottom dresser drawer and pulled out the present I'd bought for him—a bluish-green Shetland sweater, the exact color of his eyes. I'd returned two others before I'd found this one. The first looked too big when I got it home and the second itched when I tried it on. This one was just right. I took the top off the box and held the sweater to my face. It smelled new. But would it be fair to wait until his birthday—would it be honest? No . . . I had to tell him right away.

When Erica heard about my parents and the summer job in New Hampshire she canceled her plans to spend the weekend at the beach with her family and asked me over instead. I thanked her for understanding and she said, "That's what friends are for . . . remember?"

"Why don't you invite her to stay with us instead?" Mom asked when I said I was going to keep Erica company while her parents were away.

"No . . . I'd rather go there."

On Saturday night Michael and Artie came over to Erica's for supper. We fixed hotdogs and beans, a whole package of spinach for Michael and a grilled cheese sandwich for me. Erica's dog, Rex, sat under the table and she fed him scraps from her plate. Both of us were careful not to bring up the subject of summer. Artie was in one of his high moods, entertaining us with family stories until I brought out the cupcake with the candle on it and set it down in front of Michael. I sang "Happy Birthday," even though his birthday isn't until next Thursday. He was surprised and pleased and made me help him blow out the candle, at which point Artie grew very somber. "Eighteen years . . ." he said. "A quarter of our lives gone by . . . over . . . kaput . . . just like that . . ." He snapped his fingers. "From now on it's all downhill . . ."

"No, it's not," I said, "it's just the beginning . . . the best part is still coming . . ."

Artie said, "Sure . . . you spend your whole life trying to make it and for what . . . so you can wind up in some cancer ward full of needles and tubes with nobody giving a shit . . . that's what you've got to look forward to . . . that's what we've all got coming . . ."

Erica touched his arm. "You've got to enjoy whatever you can and forget about the rest."

"The odds are stacked against us . . ."

"Please, Artie . . ." I said, "don't spoil tonight."

"Hell, I'm not about to spoil it."

"Good." Erica jumped up to clear away the plates. "How about a game of dirty word Scrabble?"

"Sounds good to me," Michael said.

"Why not?" Artie asked. "Let's enjoy it while we can."

He snapped out of his glum mood and we had

a fun game, then Michael and I went to the
guest room and Erica and Artie headed upstairs,
with Rex following them.

Michael took a long time getting me ready,
or else it just seemed that way, and it worked
out very well. We don't turn out all the lights
anymore. It's much nicer being able to see as
you make love. After, while we rested, I tried
to think of how to tell him about the summer.
Finally I decided there was no easy way and I
said, "Michael . . . there's something I've got to
tell you."

"Umm . . ." he said, playing with my hair.

"Are you listening?"

"Umm . . ." His eyes were still closed.

"It's about the summer . . ." I waited for
some reaction from him. "You see . . . my parents . . . they arranged . . ." I sat up. "Oh
God . . . I don't know how to tell you this . . ."

He opened his eyes and sat up too. "Just say
it, Kath. Whatever it is . . . just say it."

"I've got to go to New Hampshire for seven
weeks . . . my father got me this job at Jamie's
camp . . . they needed an assistant tennis
counselor . . . I said no . . . I told them to forget
it . . . but they said I have no choice . . . they're
making me go, Michael . . . but I figure you
could drive up at least once, maybe twice, because I'm sure I'll get some time off . . . and
. . ." I looked over at him. "I know what you're
thinking," I said, "that I'm eighteen . . . that
I should be more independent . . . I should have

asserted myself . . . but, I don't know . . ." I stopped for a minute. "Say something, will you . . ."

"I've got a job too . . . in North Carolina."

"Oh, come on . . ."

"It's true. My uncle's got a lumber yard there and he's offered me a job for the summer . . . good pay and no expenses. I'll be staying with them."

He was serious. He was actually going to North Carolina. "How long have you known?"

"About three weeks."

I took a deep breath. "When were you going to tell me?"

"Tonight."

"Oh, sure . . ."

"I was . . ."

"You expect me to believe that?"

"It's the truth."

"I'll bet . . ."

"Look . . . I didn't want to tell you before because I kept hoping something else would turn up . . . some great job around here . . . and besides, I didn't want to think about facing the summer without you . . . if you don't believe me you can ask Artie . . . he knew I was going to tell you tonight . . ."

"You shouldn't have waited . . . that wasn't honest."

"Okay . . . so maybe I was wrong . . . I'm sorry if I was . . ."

"Whose idea was it . . . going to North Carolina?"

"Whose do you think?"

"Your parents?"

"You guessed it."

"Same here."

"So they'll find out that separating us won't change anything . . . and then maybe they'll leave us alone."

I nodded.

"Come here, Kath . . ."

I leaned over and kissed him. "We still have all of June," I said.

"I know . . . and we're going to make the most of it."

"Starting now?" I asked, kissing him again.

"Starting now . . ."

But Ralph wouldn't get hard. Even when I held him nothing happened.

"What's wrong?" I asked.

"I don't know!" Michael turned away from me. "Shit . . . this is just what I need . . ."

"Don't worry," I said, ". . . it's probably nothing." I ran my hands up and down his back. "Relax . . . it doesn't matter."

He rolled over, but Ralph stayed small and soft. Michael pushed my hand away. "Cut it out, will you . . . can't you see it's not going to work again tonight."

"Okay . . ." I said, "let's forget it."

We dressed side by side, not talking or laugh-

ing the way we usually do. I stripped the bed
and put the sheets inside the pillow case.

Erica and Artie were sitting in the living
room, waiting for us.

"You ready?" Michael asked Artie.

"Yeah."

"Let's get going then."

Erica just sat in the chair looking straight
ahead. She and Artie didn't say goodnight to
each other.

"I'll call you," Michael told me, without our
usual goodnight kiss.

"Okay," I said. I walked him to the front door
and when he and Artie were outside I saw
Michael toss him the car keys. "I hope you don't
mind driving because I've got a headache that's
not to be believed."

"Take two aspirin," I called, but he didn't
hear. I shut the door and went upstairs. Erica
was on her bed, crying. "What is it?" I asked.
I'd never seen her cry. Rex tried to lick her face.

"Everything . . . I just can't take it anymore."

"But Erica . . ."

"I've given him almost five months of my
life! And I can't help him, Kath . . . it's no
use . . . tonight was the end . . . I'm not going
to see him again."

"Come on . . ." I said. "You're just upset.
Everything will seem better in the morning."

That only made Erica cry harder. I found a
tissue box and sat by her side.

"He locked himself in my bathroom and

threatened to kill himself and I was scared he meant it . . . I was so scared . . . so I ran downstairs to get you and Michael but just as I was about to knock I heard you . . ." she was sobbing harder and harder.

"Please try to calm down, Erica . . . this isn't doing you any good."

"And then," she said, "when I got back to my room . . . there he was . . . sitting on the bed, all dressed, like nothing had happened and neither one of us said anything for the longest time and then I finally told him I don't want to see him anymore. And he looked right at me and he said, *I understand, Erica—you've been very kind and patient and I certainly don't blame you* . . . like he was acting a part in a play."

"You'll both change your minds," I said. "You'll see."

"No . . . it's over . . . don't you understand . . . it's over for good . . . and in a way I'm even glad."

19

On Thursday morning, Michael's birthday, Artie hung himself from the shower curtain rod in his bathroom. Luckily, the rod broke and he fell into the tub, winding up with a concussion and an assortment of cuts and bruises. He was stitched up at Overlook, then transferred to Carrier Clinic, a private psychiatric hospital near Princeton.

Both Michael and Erica blamed themselves. Neither one of them believed me when I said that maybe this was the best thing that could have happened because now, at least, Artie will get the kind of professional help he's needed all along.

Michael said he should have listened on Saturday night, when Artie was driving home. "He wanted to talk . . . I knew it but I didn't care . . . I was so wrapped up in my own problems I pretended to sleep all the way to my house. I wish I had it to do over again . . . I'd listen this time."

Erica was convinced it was all her fault. Wednesday afternoon, when she got home from school, Artie was parked out front, waiting for her. She told him that she'd meant what she'd said on Saturday night, and even though she still liked him as a person and always would, they were through and she didn't want him coming around anymore. "I shouldn't have ended it that way," she said. "I should have waited . . ."

We weren't in the mood to celebrate but I gave Michael his birthday present anyway. On the card I wrote, *To keep you warm next winter . . . until we can be together.* And I signed it, *Forever, Kath.*

"It's perfect," he said. "I'll wear it every day."

The next night Michael and Erica got drunk. The three of us went to The Playground, this singles bar on Route 22. We flashed our new I.D. cards at the bartender and ordered a round of screwdrivers. But even with her I.D. the bartender refused to serve Erica until she'd shown him her driver's license and her birth certificate, which she carries in her bag at all times.

Michael and Erica belted their drinks down and ordered a second round while I sipped my first slowly, the way my father said I should. After that I stuck to ginger ale. In less than two hours Michael and Erica each polished off another three drinks and were acting really dumb, singing school songs and laughing hysterically. Finally, I threatened to walk out and drive home myself if they wouldn't leave then and there.

Getting them to the car was another story. Neither one of them could walk and if it hadn't been for this very nice guy who offered to help we might still be there.

Erica got sick first, in the parking lot. When she was done we got her into the back seat of the car, where Michael was slumped in the corner. I thanked my friend and said goodbye. "Good luck," he told me. I waved. A few miles down the highway Michael heaved all over Erica, but she was so out of it she didn't even notice.

I brought them back to my house since I didn't know what else to do. My mother and father were very generous about helping them, because the truth is, they looked and smelled disgusting. Mom put Erica under the shower while Dad hosed off both Michael and his car. I made a pot of coffee.

I'd been very cool to my parents since the camp scene, but watching them help my friends, knowing that they cared, made me glad I hadn't done anything stupid.

Dad called the Wagners and the Smalls and explained the situation to them. We got Michael to bed in the den and Erica to bed in my room. Then I went to the bathroom, sat down on the toilet, and cried.

20

June—the month most seniors live for—the end of one life and the beginning of another. I read that once, on the cover of a paperback. And in a way it's true. I'd be lying if I said I wasn't caught up in the mood myself.

Yesterday I did something I've never done before. I cut all my afternoon classes. Michael picked me up right after lunch. His mother and father had gone up to the Shakespeare Festival at Stratford. We spent the rest of the day in his bed. We had no trouble with Ralph this time and I could tell that Michael was relieved. So was I. Somehow I thought I might have been to blame . . .

We didn't go to Michael's prom or mine. We'd talked about making one or the other, with Artie and Erica, but now it didn't seem right. Artie's parents told Michael there was no chance he'd be home for graduation. They asked him to write Artie short, cheerful notes, but not to expect any answers.

Jamie baked a special cake for Mom's fortieth birthday. We hid the layers in the downstairs freezer last week and defrosted them this morning, so they'd be ready to decorate when we got home from school. Jamie's icing flowers are better than any bakery's. We'd also chipped in for a big, beautiful plant that looks something like a palm tree. I drove down to the greenhouse to pick it up while Jamie put the finishing touches on the cake. I guess from now on I'll feel uneasy about birthday celebrations but as I helped Jamie get ready for Mom's party I tried to think of only happy things.

Grandma and Grandpa sent forty yellow tea roses, enough to fill up every vase in the house, plus a check. We had a really nice dinner and Mom got tears in her eyes when Jamie and I carried in her cake, singing "Happy Birthday." Then we gave her the plant. She loved it.

Dad's official present to her was a chunky silver bracelet she'd picked out in Mexico but he handed her a surprise package too—inside was a pink and orange bikini. She laughed when she saw it, kissed him, and told us it was great to be forty—that it sounded much worse than it felt. I wished Artie could have been there to see her.

Later, Mom tried on her new bikini and modeled it for us. When she came to my room she said, "Tell the truth, Kath . . . are my thighs getting flabby?"

I said, "No . . . of course not."

"Then what's this?" she asked, squeezing some extra flesh.

I didn't come right out and say it was flab. I told her, "I can teach you some exercises to get rid of it."

"I may take you up on that," she said. "And Kath . . . thank you for a lovely birthday."

"Any time," I answered.

The phone rang that night at 11:30. We never get calls that late because everyone knows my parents sack out early. I heard my father answer and say, ". . . just a minute . . . I'll see . . ."

He came to my door. "Are you awake?" he asked.

"Half . . . who is it?"

"Erica."

"At this hour?"

"She says it's important."

"Okay . . . I'll take it downstairs."

I picked up the phone in the kitchen and yawned. "Hello . . ."

"Sybil had a baby girl!"

I came awake very fast. "She did . . . when?"

"Tonight . . . her mother just called . . . six pounds, one ounce."

"But it's only the middle of June."

"I know . . . she was two weeks early."

"Is she okay?"

"Fine . . . so's the baby."

"I'm glad."

"Me too . . . see you tomorrow."

Erica and I went to visit Sybil in the hospital. Instead of going directly to her room we stopped off at the nursery first. Babies are on view twice a day, during afternoon and evening visiting hours. You can watch them through the glass wall. Sybil's baby had a headful of black hair and was fast asleep.

"What do you think?" Erica asked.

"She's very small."

"They all are."

"Yeah . . . I guess so."

"Do you think she looks like Sybil?" Erica said.

"I can't tell . . . they're not at their best until they're a few months old."

"I know . . . new ones look all shriveled up and distorted."

"I suppose if it's yours, you feel different," I said.

"Do you think just having a baby automatically makes you love it?"

"I'm not sure . . . you might have to learn to love it, like any other person."

We brought Sybil a bouquet of daisies. I arranged them in a disposable vase, the way I do when I'm working at the hospital. She was expecting us since Erica had phoned earlier to make sure she wanted company.

"Hi . . ." she said, and before either one of us had a chance to say anything she began to talk. "I want you to know it was no big deal . . . those movies showing women screaming in labor are plain bullshit . . . there's nothing to it . . . you just push and push and finally the baby pops out . . . to tell you the truth I don't even remember that much about it except there was this very nice guy standing over me and every time a strong contraction started he gave me a whiff of gas . . . did you see her yet? Isn't she adorable? Oh, thanks for the daisies . . . I love daisies . . . you know tonight's my graduation . . . I really planned to be there . . . but you can't fight Mother Nature . . . they're going to mail me my diploma . . . did I tell you I've decided to take off fifty pounds and go to Smith?"

She stopped to take a breath and Erica and I looked at each other.

"I'm getting an IUD so I won't get pregnant again because I've no intention of giving up sex . . . but the next time I have a baby I want to make sure I can keep it . . . did you see how much hair she has? My mother says it will probably all fall out and her regular hair will be completely different." She sighed, then smiled at us. "Thanks for coming. I'm glad you did. Are you going to Michael's graduation?" She directed this question to me.

"Yes."

"Then you'll hear them call my name."

"I'll clap for you . . . okay?"

"Sure . . . for me and Artie," Sybil said. Then she looked up at Erica and shook her head. "I'm sorry."

"It's okay."

"I'd rather be here than where he is," Sybil said.

"When are you coming home?" Erica asked.

"Day after tomorrow . . . but I'm supposed to take it easy for a week or two after that."

"Maybe you'll come to the the beach with us . . ."

"Maybe . . . the baby leaves on Friday with her adoptive parents . . . I hope she has a good life . . ." Sybil reached for a tissue and blew her nose. I hoped she wouldn't cry. I already had a lump in my throat.

"I figure two people who really want a kid will take good care of her . . . don't you think?"

"Sure," Erica said, "it's the best way."

"It's not like I could keep her . . . that wouldn't be fair . . ."

"You're doing the right thing," I told her, wondering why she hadn't thought about all that before.

"Are you sleeping with Michael?" she suddenly asked me.

"That's a very personal question," I answered.

She nodded. "I could have had an abortion but I wanted the experience of giving birth."

"Could have . . . should have . . ." Erica

said, "it doesn't matter now . . . what's done is done."

"I've asked to see the baby one more time," Sybil told us, brightening. "The doctor said I can give her a bottle tonight . . . I hope they name her Jennifer . . ."

21

It was a beautiful, clear night and Michael's graduation was held outside. I sat with Sharon and Ike and finally met Michael's parents. His mother took my hand and said, "Well, at last . . . we've heard so much about you." She had red hair and freckles and wore eye make-up.

His father said, "So you're Katherine . . ."

And I told him, "Yes, I am."

He had a beer belly and a lot of grayish hair and a nice voice, deep, like a disc jockey's.

I choked up when Sybil's name was called, when Artie's wasn't, but should have been, and again when it was Michael's turn to accept his diploma. I kept dabbing my eyes, pretending I had something in one of them, in case Sharon or Ike were wondering.

After graduation there was a party at Michael's, a kind of Open House in the back yard, for his relatives. His mother introduced me to everyone as "Michael's little friend." I didn't much care for that but I wasn't about to say anything.

Sharon handed me a glass of champagne. "I hear you're going to be a tennis counselor this summer."

"Just an assistant."

"Sounds like fun. I'd love to get away for a while."

"What about your trip?"

"That fell through. I can't leave my job right now."

"Oh, that's too bad."

"There'll be other opportunities . . ."

I sipped my drink. Some of the bubbles went up my nose.

Ike said, "I like your hair that way."

"It's the same as always," I told him.

"Oh . . . I guess I never noticed." We each took a little hotdog in a blanket as Michael's mother passed with a tray. "You're graduating too, aren't you?" Ike asked.

"Thursday night." I had to answer with my mouth half open because the hotdog was burning my tongue.

"Well . . . congratulations in advance."

"Thank you."

Sharon wandered off and an uncle of Michael's joined us. "I hear you're going to Denver," he said.

I nodded and finished my champagne.

"Wonderful city . . . plenty of sunshine . . . fresh air . . ."

"Excuse me," Ike said, and left me alone with him.

"You have a lot to look forward to."

"Yes, I know," I said. "You're not from North Carolina, by any chance, are you?"

"No . . . that's my brother, Stephen."

"Oh." I looked around for Michael.

The uncle picked something out of his teeth, examined it, then flicked it off his finger. "So tell me," he said, "what do you want to do with your life?"

"Do?" I repeated.

"Yes . . . you've thought about it, haven't you?"

"Sure."

"So?"

"I want to be happy," I told him. "And make other people happy too."

"Very nice . . . but not enough."

"That's all I know right now." I turned and walked away from him.

My parents were asleep when Michael and I got to my house. We locked ourselves into the den, took off our clothes and held each other.

"Let's lie down on the rug," I said.

Michael looked at it. We were used to the sofa.

"For old time's sake . . ."

"Sure," he said, "why not . . ."

We stretched out on it, kissing. "Remember

the first night we were together on the rug . . . with the fire . . ."

"And Erica and Artie in the other room . . ." Michael said.

"Yes . . . and after you left and Erica had gone upstairs I sat on the rug for a while thinking that it was very special . . . that it was ours . . ." I kissed his ears, running my tongue around the edges. I used my hands on his body while I worked my way down, kissing his neck, his chest, his belly.

"You're aggressive tonight . . ."

I hadn't thought about that until he said it. I was surprised myself. "Do you mind?"

"I like it."

I lay on top of him, feeling Ralph against my stomach. "Can we try it this way?" I whispered.

"Any way you want," he said.

I straddled him, helping Ralph find the right angle, and when he was inside me I moved slowly—up, down and around—up, down and around—until I couldn't control myself anymore. "Oh, God . . . oh, Michael . . . now . . . now . . ." And then I came. I came before he did. But I kept moving until he groaned and as he finished I came again, not caring about anything—anything but how good it felt.

"Happy graduation . . ." I laughed. After, we lay in each other's arms and I thought, there are so many ways to love a person. This is how it should be—forever.

*   *   *

My graduation was held indoors at the last minute because of a tremendous thunderstorm that began at 4:30 and lasted for hours, on and off. Each senior was allowed only two tickets for an indoor graduation so Michael had to wait for me at home, with Jamie and my grandparents. He didn't get to see me in my cap and gown.

We had a party at our house too, with a table full of sandwiches, fresh fruits and a big chocolate graduation cake.

The next morning Michael and I left for Long Beach Island. We'd been invited to Erica's house at Loveladies Harbor. It's a two hour trip from Westfield, straight down the parkway. We took turns driving.

Erica's house stands on stilts, right on the beach. From the outside it looks like three boxes —a big one in the middle and two smaller ones on either side. The side of the house facing the ocean is all glass. There's a large living room with a white tile floor and white wicker furniture with green cushions. Then there are two smaller wings, each with two bedrooms and a bathroom. Mr. and Mrs. Small use one wing for themselves. Erica's room is in the other. I was sharing with her and Michael's room was opposite ours. None of us mentioned Artie or the fact that we'd planned this weekend long ago, for the four of us.

After lunch we walked up and down the beach, tossing a football around. Erica introduced us to all the summer kids—she's known them for ages. There's a surfing beach a few miles down, in Harvey Cedars, and we sat there for a while, watching a couple of guys trying to catch a wave. We used up a roll of film posing on their surfboards.

That night, after dark, most of the kids we'd met earlier dropped by. One girl brought her guitar and sang for us. Some kids smoked grass but I didn't want to, so Michael drank beer instead, but not enough to get sick. And later, when everyone had gone home and Erica went to bed, Michael and I took a sleeping bag out to the beach and we made love. We woke up at dawn and watched the sun come up together.

Four days later Jamie and I left for camp.

22

Wednesday
June 26

Dear Michael,

Here I am at camp! The bus ride up was bad news. The air conditioning broke after an hour and we sweltered the rest of the way. One kid heaved in the aisle so we had to stop and let everyone out while the staff cleaned up the mess. I am considered staff!

There are 75 campers, all between the ages of 12 and 15 and every one of them is talented in music or art or both, like Jamie. Tennis is the only organized sport here, besides waterfront. The head tennis counselor is called Theo. He told me right off that I will be teaching the kids with less ability.

The girls live in a big old house and the boys have a sleeping dorm (a converted barn) and the 15 staff members are scattered around. My room is in the house and my roommate is from Seattle. She's a weaving expert. Her name is

189

*Angela and she doesn't believe in shaving any
body hair and thinks natural body smells beat
deodorant. Don't ask!!!*

*As soon as we got here, Foxy, the director,
called a staff meeting and gave us a big lecture
about drugs, which are prohibited. As far as I
can tell that's the only rule.*

*To tell you the truth, I don't know what I'm
doing here. I wish I was with you. Only 49 days
until we can be together. I hope I live that long.*

Love forever,
Kath

Friday night
June 28

Dear Kath,

*I just got your letter. I read it eight times. I
wish I could be your roommate instead of Angela. As you know I have plenty of deodorant.
You wouldn't believe how hot it is here. It's im-
possible to breathe. I picked up my plane ticket
today. I leave Wednesday night. Yesterday I ran
into Erica. We were both ordering sandwiches
to go at the Robert Treat Deli. There are a lot
of things I would like to tell you but I'm not very
good at writing them down. If you were here I'd
show you what I mean. I guess you get the
picture.*

I miss you so much!

Love forever,
Michael

P.S. Ralph also misses you.

Monday
July 1

Dear Michael,

I hope you get this before you leave. It rained all day today. This morning I was assigned a co-ed modern dance group. They weren't bad—I was really surprised. I slept all afternoon and I feel better now. I've been so tired since I got here. Do you know it's been eight days since we've been together!!! *I'm trying hard not to think about that because every time I do I miss you more and more. I have all your pictures taped on the wall above my bed. Angela says you're very natural looking. I think that's supposed to be a compliment. I didn't tell her that you usually wear eyeshadow and color your hair. Ha ha.*

Yesterday I waterskied and fell down in the middle of the lake. I almost lost my bathing suit. Luckily, only Kerrie was in the boat. She's Australian and is in charge of water sports with her husband, Poe.

Jamie says hello.

Have a safe trip to North Carolina but Do Not talk to any strangers on the plane, especially female ones. And don't forget that I love you! And that I miss you more than I can say.

Forever,
Kath

July 2
Tuesday night

Dear Kath,

I'm so excited! I wrote an editorial for The
Leader *and it's going to be printed in next week's
issue. It deals with senior year. I'll send you a
copy. I'm leaving for the beach tomorrow night
for Fourth of July weekend. Sybil's coming too.*

*I ran into Michael at the Robert Treat a few
days ago and tonight I saw him at Friendly's.
We had an ice cream together and talked about
you. He's all packed and ready to go. I kissed
him goodbye for you—very platonically—on the
cheek. I'm going to miss both of you this summer.*

*I'm enclosing Artie's address at the clinic.
Michael said you asked for it. I wish I had it to
do all over again with him. I'd handle things a
lot differently. Oh well—as my mother says, we
grow from our experiences. I hope that's true.*

Have fun.

                    Love,
                    Erica

July 2

Dear Mom and Dad,

*I guess you could say I'm adjusting to camp.
Most of the staff is very nice. I like Nan, the
photography counselor, best. Theo, the head of
the tennis program, calls me Kat, even though I
have explained at least a million times that*

nobody calls me that. I got a letter from Grand-ma. I didn't know they were going to Martha's Vineyard next week. Did Jamie write that she has a new boyfriend? His name is Stuart. If she hasn't told you don't let on that you know. She'd kill me! He plays the oboe and has braces on his teeth. I never knew you could play that kind of instrument wearing braces. He's very good.

Last night Foxy called a special staff meeting telling us that the emphasis here is supposed to be on friendship, not sex! Don't worry about Jamie, though. I'm keeping an eye on her. Besides, Stuart is more interested in his oboe than in her.

See you on visiting day.

> *Love,*
> *Kath*

July 3
Wednesday

Dear Kath,

I'm at the airport waiting to board my plane. Don't worry about strange girls. I'm scared of them! Oh-oh . . . they just announced my flight. Have to run. I love you. I'm counting the days too. Only 42 more.

> *Forever,*
> *Michael*

P.S. Keep that bathing suit on (until I get back).

Thurs. July 4

Dear Artie,

I'm an assistant tennis counselor at the camp in New Hampshire where my sister, Jamie, goes. It's not a bad job. The lake is really beautiful, but cold. I hope you're feeling okay. Just wanted to let you know I'm thinking of you.

Your friend,
Kath

Friday, July 5

Dear Erica,

When you get this you'll be back from the beach. I hope you had a good weekend. I wish you'd find a nice guy and get Artie off your mind. You can't go on blaming yourself forever. Remember your vow to get laid before college? Well, I've been thinking about that and I've decided it might be just what you need. And you know I wouldn't say that if I really didn't mean it.

You should see me. I'm a mess. My nose and forehead are peeling like mad. It's been very hot since Tuesday and I broil on the courts four hours a day. But that's better than at night—because at least my mind is occupied. Nights are the worst. You just don't know what it's like for me, trying not to think of Michael . . . knowing that we're going to be apart for so long. It's pure torture.

But here's some good news! My roommate, Angela, the smelly one, has moved in with Zack, the potter. He has a shack on the grounds. So now I have a room all to myself.

Most of the kids here are okay. There's just one 15 year old brat I can't stand. Her name is Marsha. Everyone says she's a fantastic ballerina but I haven't seen her dance yet. She's too busy hanging around the tennis courts because of Theo. When I compare us at 15 to Marsha, I can see that times are really changing . . . and not for the better, in my opinion. I wouldn't want to see Jamie carrying on like that in two years.

I'll say this for Theo—he's not impressed by silly kids. He doesn't say much about himself but my friend, Nan, knows that he is 21 and a senior at Northwestern. Nan is impossibly shy around guys but I'm going to try to fix things up between the two of them. He's not as bad as I first thought.

Time for supper now. Write soon.

> *Love,*
> *Kath*

> *July 9*
> *Tuesday*

Dear Kath,

We had a great weekend at the beach. The weather was perfect. I think I told you that Sybil was coming with us. She's on another one of her diets but this time with the doctor's approval. She didn't want to talk about the baby.

I think the whole experience was more than she bargained for.

Thanks for your suggestions. But I've been doing a lot of thinking and have decided I don't want to fuck just for the hell of it. I want it to be special, like you and Michael. So I'm going to wait.

Theo and Nan sound nice. I'm glad you've found some friends. They should help make the time go faster.

Love,
Erica

Thursday, July 11

Dear Kath,

Dad and I enjoy hearing from you very much. We're glad you're adjusting to camp. It's been very hot here. Yesterday the air conditioning in the library broke down and we had to close early.

Let me know if there's anything you need on visiting day. We're looking forward to spending the day with you and Jamie. Grandma and Grandpa are off to Martha's Vineyard for ten days. Erica stopped in the library to say hello. That's about it.

Love,
Mom

23

The campers have to report to their rooms at 10:00 every night. Then the staff gets together in the retreat, which is a small cottage with some comfortable furniture. Usually I write my letters there.

Sometimes, while I'm trying to think of what to say I'll look up for a minute and catch Theo watching me. He doesn't get embarrassed and turn away but I do. His eyes are light green and Nan says every time she looks into them she melts. His hair is brown and hangs into his face. On the courts he has to wear a headband to keep it away so he can see the ball. He's got a moustache that turns down around the corners of his mouth and he's very tan, including his back and chest, because he hardly ever wears a shirt.

The other day, Theo, Nan and I were on the dock. I laughed when he took off his socks and sneakers because his feet were so white. So he picked me up and tossed me into the lake. I was wearing jeans and a shirt and I wanted to kill him.

The truth is, he's not the wise-ass I thought he was going to be when we first met. He's very patient with the kids and is even helping me improve my game. Sometimes, after dinner, we play a set or two. He says I'm the only one here who can give him a decent workout.

One night, during the first week of camp, Theo came over and pointed to my necklace. "What's it say?" he asked.

"This . . ." I said, holding up the disk.

"Yes."

"It says *Katherine* on one side and *Michael* on the other."

"The guy you're always writing to?"

"Uh huh."

"Can I see?"

"Sure."

He stood very close to me and took it in his hand. He looked at the side that said *Katherine* first, then turned it over. "What's *forever* supposed to mean?"

"What do you think?" I asked.

"I think forever's one hell of a long time for a kid like you."

"I'm not a kid. I happen to be eighteen."

"Congratulations," he said.

Right after that I asked him to please stop calling me Kat.

He said, "I can't stop now . . . I'm used to it . . . besides, it suits you."

Now everyone at camp calls me Kat. I don't mind as much as I did then.

I got a letter from Michael.

Dear Kath,

   I'm getting settled here. I've got my own room since my cousin, Danny, is away for the summer. His twin sisters are thirteen and remind me of Jamie. Tell her I said hello. I'm getting to be a first rate lumber stacker. Next week I get to work the saw. That's a big step up! I think about you every night—all night.

Love forever,
Michael

Dear Michael,

   Be careful with the saw! I don't want anything to happen to your hands. I love them (and the rest of you isn't bad either). Ha ha.

Love forever,
Kath

Each staff member gets two short and one long night off each week. A long night means you don't have to hang around for evening activity. You can leave right after supper and you don't have to report in until the next morning.

This week Theo asked if Nan and I would like to go into Laconia with him to see a movie. He has a car and we don't. Naturally we accepted.

I tried to arrange it so that I would sit next to

Nan and she would sit between me and Theo
but he decided it was only fair that he sit in the
middle, since he was the only guy. He put one
arm around each of us but I knew it was just a
joke. It's funny, the way you get to know summer friends so well in a short period of time,
especially at camp, when you are thrown together morning, noon and night.

Sometimes I dream that Michael and I are
making love. I can understand that. But in the
middle of the night after the movie, I woke up
drenched with perspiration and ashamed—more
ashamed than I've ever been in my life. I
dreamed I was with Theo. It was so real—I
could smell him, taste him, feel him—and I
wanted him so much. I did things to him that I
have only read about.

I wrote Michael a four-page letter the next
day, to keep my mind where it belongs. I stayed
as far away from Theo as I could. Even so, I
knew there was something growing between us.
Something I was afraid to even think about.

Every night, from 8:00 to 10:00, the canteen
is open and the campers can hang out in there,
listening to music, dancing and getting snacks.
Theo dances with the younger kids, like Jamie,
but avoids the older ones, like Marsha. You can
tell he's not looking for trouble. Nan doesn't
dance at all. She says she has two left feet. That
presents a real problem because dancing can be
a very good way to get two people together. And
Theo likes to dance. If only he would look at

Nan the way he looks at me. If only my insides didn't turn over every time our eyes meet.

Tonight, Marsha put on this slow song and all the kids booed her because they prefer hard rock. They don't even know how to touch-dance. But Marsha wouldn't change the record and she came slithering over to Theo and tried to drag him to his feet. He told her, "Sorry, Marsha . . . but I promised this one to Kat." And he took my hand and pulled me up. I shook my head but he didn't care. He said to the kids, "Watch carefully . . . and I'll show you a new way to dance." Then he put his arms around me and the kids whistled and cheered and Theo laughed and held me tighter. Soon, some of the kids got up to try touch-dancing and Theo started the record from the beginning again.

He's not much taller than I am—just three or four inches—and I was wearing clogs, so that as we danced our bodies came together. We didn't talk or look at each other but there was a lot going on between us. When the record ended I broke away from him and ran out of the canteen. I went down to the lake where it's cool and dark and I sat on a rock and I cried. How can you love one person and still be attracted to another?

The next day I got a long letter from Michael. I kissed it and showed it to Nan to prove that I am not the least bit interested in anyone but him.

On visiting day I spent the morning on the

courts rallying with the campers so their parents could see how much their games had improved. Foxy gave me the afternoon off to be with Mom and Dad. I was the only counselor who had visitors. After lunch Jamie showed them her oils and watercolors and the fabric she's weaving with Angela's help. Then my father changed into tennis shorts and he and I played two sets. I beat him 6-3, 7-5. He was very impressed.

Later, I took Mom up to see my room. "It's nice and cozy." She sat on my bed and looked at the pictures of Michael taped to the wall. "You seem to be getting along very well . . . I'm glad."

"I'm managing . . ." I told her. I went to my closet and took out a shoe box full of letters. "Look at this," I said, ". . . all from Michael. We write every day."

Mom nodded.

"I'll bet you thought we wouldn't."

"No . . . I never thought that."

24

On the following Sunday night I was in the retreat answering Erica's letter, when Foxy poked his head in and said there was a phone call for me. I looked at my watch. It was 10:30. Who would call me at 10:30?

Nan walked me over to the office.

My mother was on the line.

I said, "Mom . . . what's wrong?"

She said, "Bad news, Kath . . ."

"What is it?" I felt tears in my eyes before I even knew.

"It's Grandpa, honey . . ."

"What . . .?"

"Another stroke . . . he didn't make it this time, Kath. He died two hours ago."

"No . . ." I said and I started to cry for real. "No!"

"Yes, Kath . . . I'm sorry I have to tell you this way . . ." Her voice trailed off and my father got on. "Kath?"

I couldn't talk.

"Kath . . . are you still there?"

I made a small noise.

"Listen, Kath . . . he didn't suffer . . . he just passed out and when they got him to the hospital he was gone."

"Dead?"

"Yes . . . dead."

"Oh, Daddy . . . I didn't want him to die . . ."

"None of us did . . . but we didn't want him to suffer either."

"But he was so nice . . . so good . . ."

"I know . . ."

"What about Grandma?"

"She's okay."

"I want to talk to Mom again."

"Kath . . ." Mom said.

"I want to come home," I told her, "right away . . . I want to be with you and Grandma . . . I'll pack tonight and leave first thing in the morning."

"No, honey . . . we've talked it over and we don't want you to come home."

"But I have to . . ."

"Please listen . . . Grandpa didn't want a funeral . . . you know that . . . If you stay at camp with Jamie for another ten days Grandma will have a chance to get herself together. She wants you to do this for her."

"Is she all right . . . you're telling me the truth, aren't you?"

"She's right upstairs . . . resting . . . Uncle Howard's with her."

"I want to talk to her."

"Tomorrow."

"What about Jamie?" I asked. "Who's going to tell her?"

"Do you think you could do it?"

"I don't know."

"Please try . . . in the morning . . . and then call us."

"Okay . . . I'll try."

"Get some sleep now . . . and we'll talk tomorrow."

"Tell Grandma I'm sorry . . . will you?"

"I will."

"I loved him."

"We all did."

I told Nan what had happened and that I needed to be alone for a while. I went down to the lake and sat on my rock and I thought about Grandpa. I remembered how he'd played horsey with me when I was just a little kid and how he'd read aloud, using a different voice for each character. I thought of him sniffing around in the kitchen when Jamie and Grandma were preparing their feasts. I thought of how he'd looked after his first stroke—small and white and how he'd held out his hand to me when I visited him in the hospital. I tried to remember all the good things—the way he'd toasted Grandma in the restaurant—*To love,* he'd said, raising his glass.

And then I got the feeling I wasn't alone any-more. I turned away from the lake and saw Theo.

"Nan told me," he said. "I'm really sorry."

"He was very special . . . you just don't know . . ." I buried my face in my hands and I cried.

Theo sat on the grass, beside me. "It's hard to accept death," he said.

"He's the first person I've loved who's died."

"It's hard the first time."

"I don't know what to do," I told him.

He didn't talk until I was all cried out. Then he said, "I think you should get some rest now."

"I don't want to," I said. "I don't want to be alone."

"Maybe you could stay with Nan."

I shook my head.

"You can't sit here all night, Kat."

"I have to tell Jamie in the morning . . . how do you tell that to someone?"

"The simplest way possible."

"I'm not sure I'll be able to."

"I'll come with you if you want . . . but right now you've got to get to bed." He stood up and took my hand. "I'll walk you back to the house."

When we got there he smoothed my hair away from my face. "Goodnight, Kat . . ." he said, kissing my forehead.

I put my arms around him and pulled him close and I kissed him, the way I had in my dream, and at first he kissed me back—then he untangled himself from me and said, "Not like this . . . not with death for an excuse."

I ran to my room and started crying all over again.

It was a mistake to tell Jamie about Grandpa after breakfast. She threw up as soon as she heard. But all in all she took it better than I did and she didn't want to go home. We called Mom and Dad and I asked to talk to Grandma.

"We had forty-seven wonderful years to-gether," she told me. "How many people can match that?"

"Not many," I said. Hearing her voice made me feel better.

July 28

Dear Michael,

My grandfather died yesterday. He had an-other stroke. There's not going to be any funeral. He wanted to be cremated. I spoke to my grand-mother this morning and she's okay. She's asked me to stay at camp with Jamie even though I want to go home and be with her. I won't be-lieve this really happened until I get back and see that Grandpa's not there anymore. I'm going to miss him so much.

        Love,
        Kath

A few nights later Nan went into town with Kerrie and Poe but Theo stayed at camp with me, even though he had the night off too. We sat together on the steps of his cabin.

"About the other night . . ." he began.

But I told him, "I'd rather not talk about it."

"You have to, Kat."

I shook my head.

"You needed to be close to someone," he said, "and I happened to be handy." He kicked at the ground with his foot. "Sex is an antidote to death . . . did you know that?"

"No."

"Psychology Two . . . it's a very common reaction . . . somebody dies . . . you need to prove you're alive . . . and what better way is there?"

"I'm not sure that's how it was," I said.

He stood up, then went down to the lake and tossed in a few stones. I thought of that first day I'd spent with Michael.

"Look," he said, as if he could read my mind, "what about this *forever* business?"

I turned away but he walked up to me, put his hands on my shoulders and made me face him. "I want to see you again . . . after camp . . . but I won't until you get your head together."

"I need to think," I said.

July 31

Dear Kath,

 I'm really sorry about your grandfather. I liked him a lot. I wish I could be with you because it's hard for me to let you know I under-

stand this way. Soon we'll be together. I love you and miss you.

> *Forever,*
> *Michael*

I couldn't answer that letter.

August 4

Dear Kath,
I haven't heard from you. Is everything okay? Did you get my last letter? I meant what I said.
> *Love forever,*
> *Michael*

Dear Michael,
No, everything is not okay—but it's not your fault. I don't know how to say this but I'm going to try. I think I still love you but something's changed. I've met someone who's got me very mixed up. No, that's not exactly true. I mean it's true that I'm mixed up, but I can't blame him for that. I know this is hard for you to understand. It's hard for me, too. I made promises to you that I'm not sure I can keep. None of it has anything to do with you. It's just that I don't know what to do now. You must be thinking what a rotten person I am. Well, believe me, I'm thinking the same thing. I don't know how this happened or why. Maybe I can get over it. Do you think you can wait—because I don't want you to stop loving me. I keep remember-

ing us and how it was. I don't want to hurt you . . . not ever . . .

I couldn't finish. Tears were stinging my eyes. Maybe there's something wrong with me. I don't know. Maybe if Michael and I had been together for the summer this never would have happened . . .

Later, when I read the letter over, I knew I could never send it. I ripped it into tiny pieces and threw them away.

25

On Saturday afternoon, right before activities ended, I was called to the office. Theo told the kids on the courts to rally by themselves and he walked me over, holding my hand, sensing how scared I was. Please don't let it be Grandma, I prayed . . . please don't let it be anything bad this time.

When we got there Foxy looked up from his desk and said, "Hi, Kat . . . you've got a visitor." He pointed to the bathroom but before I could ask any questions the door opened. And there was Michael.

Theo and I were standing side by side, both of us dressed in cut-off shorts, him with no shirt and me in a halter, covered with sweat, smudged with dirt and still holding hands, which we dropped immediately.

"Michael . . ." I said, going to him. "How can you be here?"

"I was worried," he said. "You didn't answer

my letters so I flew in a few days early and decided to surprise you."

"Well . . . you did. You really did. Look at me . . . I'm a mess!"

"Not to me, you're not."

He hugged me hard, then I introduced him to Theo and they shook hands. "I've heard a lot about you," Theo said.

"I've heard a lot about you too," Michael told him, which wasn't exactly true because I only wrote about Theo now and then and it always had something to do with Nan.

Theo said, "I'll see you later . . . I've got to get cleaned up for supper." I wasn't sure if he'd meant that for me or for Michael. He walked out of the office.

Foxy said, "You can take a long night off, Kat."

I went back to the house, stood under a hot shower and shampooed my hair, thinking, what can I say to him—how can I explain—how can I make him understand without hating me? And now that he's here—now that I've seen him again—I don't know what I want. I let the water run off my hair into my face but it wasn't just the shampoo that made my eyes burn.

I put on the only dress I'd brought to camp. Michael was waiting for me downstairs. He took my hand and we walked to his car. He drove to a restaurant on the wharf and ordered lobsters and a bottle of white wine. We talked about Grandpa and Michael pulled two obituaries out

of his pocket—one from *The New York Times*
and one from *The Leader*. Erica had written it
herself. Then we talked about North Carolina
and lumber yards and tennis and Jamie and the
weather and the food. We didn't get around to
the most important thing at dinner, but I knew
before long we would. And what then?

After dinner we went to Michael's room at the
motel. He took off his shirt—a yellow polo with
an alligator above the pocket—and tossed it
onto a chair. We sat on the bed and as we
kissed he unbuttoned my dress. All I had on
under it was a pair of bikinis. He got out of his
jeans, then his underpants. We lay side by side.
Michael pushed my dress up, kissing me all the
time. I couldn't really kiss him back. "I've missed
you so much . . ." he said, "so much . . ." I didn't
let my tongue wander into his mouth the way I
used to. I just lay there, waiting. I couldn't let
myself feel anything.

He put his hand inside my dress and held my
breasts, squeezing one, then the other. I thought
of pretending. Some people do that. They think
of other things while they're making love. They
pretend they are with other partners. He ran his
hand up the inside of my thigh, resting it between my legs. I didn't wiggle out of my bikinis.
I'm no good at pretending. And anyway, pretending isn't fair.

"Come on, Kath . . ." he whispered.

"No, wait," I said. "Wait, Michael . . ."

"I can't . . ."

I rolled away from him. "You have to." I got off the bed and crossed the room. "We've got to talk."

"I thought that's what we've been doing for the last couple of hours."

"This is different."

"You're thinking about your grandfather, aren't you?" he asked. "But he'd want us to be together . . . you don't have to feel guilty."

"That's not it."

"Then what?"

"I'm trying to explain . . . if you'll give me a chance."

"Go ahead . . . I'm listening . . ."

"Look," I told him, "it's not you. You haven't done anything . . . it's me . . . it's that . . . well . . ."

He gave me a long look, then jumped off the bed so fast he startled me. "There's another guy, isn't there?" He pulled on his underpants.

"In a way, I guess," I started to say, "but . . ."

"Did you sleep with him?"

"No . . . nothing like that."

He got into his jeans. "Then why did you have to tell me?"

"I didn't tell you . . . you guessed it . . ."

He put his shirt on inside out. "And you wanted me to, didn't you? I mean, Jesus . . . you lay there like a vegetable and I'm dumb enough to think it has to do with your grandfather . . . you must have thought I'd never catch on . . . that I'm really stupid."

"Come on, Michael . . . I don't think that and you know it. I'd have told you myself in another minute. We're supposed to be honest with each other, remember?"

"Yeah . . . I remember a lot of things . . ." He looked around for his sneakers. ". . . which is more than I can say for you."

"I haven't forgotten anything."

"No? What about forever . . . or is your memory failing at an early age?" He found his shoes and sat on the chair, putting them on but not tying the laces.

"I didn't forget . . . not about you and not about forever."

"Then what the hell's going on?"

"Please, Michael . . . don't . . ."

"Don't . . ." he shouted. "Hell, I'm not the one who's all fucked up!"

"I just don't want any lies between us."

"And you think it can be the same for us . . . now?"

"I don't know."

"Well, I'll tell you . . . it can't!" His voice broke. He went into the bathroom, slammed the door and flushed the toilet so I couldn't hear anything.

I didn't know what to do. I waited a while before I called, "Michael . . . are you okay?"

"Oh, sure . . ." he answered. "Just fine . . . just great . . ."

"Look . . . it could be that you rushed me so

tonight . . . and I was too tense . . . oh, you
know . . ."

"Don't give me any of that crap."

"It's not crap . . ."

He flushed the toilet again.

I buttoned my dress.

Finally he opened the bathroom door. His
shirt was still inside out but he'd tied his sneakers. He walked over to the nightstand and put
on his glasses. "I'm not about to share you," he
said, sounding very calm. "I want it the way it
was before . . . so make up your mind . . ."

I swallowed hard. "I can't make any promises
. . . not now."

"That's what I thought."

"Are you saying it's over, then?"

"You said it . . . just now."

"Couldn't we sit on it a little while and see
what happens?"

"You can't have it both ways."

"Then it's really over, isn't it?" Suddenly question number four popped into my mind. *Have
you thought about how this relationship will
end?*

"I guess so," he said.

I took off my necklace and held it out to him.
My throat was too tight to talk.

"Keep it," he told me.

"I don't think I should." Our fingers touched
as I handed it to him.

"What am I supposed to do with a necklace
that says *Katherine?*"

"I don't know."

He picked up my pocketbook and dropped the necklace into it.

Neither one of us said anything on the drive back to camp. When we got there I opened the car door and stepped out, and as I did he leaned over and said, "You might as well know . . . I screwed my way around North Carolina . . ."

I shook my head to show I didn't believe him.

So he shouted, "I humped everything in sight!"

"Lair!" I shouted back. "You're just saying that to hurt me."

"You'll never know though . . . will you?" He took off so fast the tires shrieked and left marks on the road.

26

We saw each other one more time before we left for school. Erica and I were shopping in Hahne's and there he was, at the stationery counter.

I said, "Hi."

And he said, "Oh . . . hi."

I said, "How are you?"

And he said, "Okay . . . and you?"

"Okay . . . how's Artie?"

"He's home. I saw him yesterday."

"I'm glad."

Erica disappeared down another aisle and Michael and I stood there, looking at each other.

"Well . . ." I said, "good luck at school."

"You too."

"Thanks."

"Oh, by the way, I got that job in Vail . . ."

"Are you going to take it?"

He shrugged. "It all depends . . ."

"Michael . . ."

"Yeah?"

I wanted to tell him that I will never be sorry for loving him. That in a way I still do—that maybe I always will. I'll never regret one single thing we did together because what we had was very special. Maybe if we were ten years older it would have worked out differently. Maybe. I think it's just that I'm not ready for forever.

I hope that Michael knew what I was thinking. I hope that my eyes got the message through to him, because all I could manage to say was, "See you around . . ."

"Yeah," he answered, "see you around."

When I got home Jamie was out back with David and my mother was pruning her birthday tree.

"It looks nice," I said. "It's getting fatter."

"It needs a lot of water," she told me. "Did you get everything at Hahne's?"

"Almost everything."

"Are you all right . . . you don't look well . . ."

"I've had better days . . . but I'm okay. I think I'll take a shower before dinner."

"Go ahead . . . and Kath . . ."

"Yes?"

"Theo called."